It was just a kiss

Sure. And Texas was just a state.

She could not—would not—fall in love with Cade McGovern.

Yet she wanted Cade in a physical and emotional way that she had never wanted anyone else in her life. A sound that was part laugh, part sob broke past her lips that still tingled from his kiss.

She forced her mind away from the man and the kiss that had left her emotions in turmoil and tried to focus. Someone had slashed the SUV's tires. The incident might have nothing to do with her, but the black market baby ring was out there somewhere, just waiting for her to surface again. Her family was probably worried sick by now. And a small part of her was terrified that the bullet had done some sort of permanent damage to her shoulder.

But none of those reasons was as compelling as her main one: She needed to leave before Cade got so far under her skin, he'd have to be surgically removed....

Dear Harlequin Intrigue Reader,

All the evidence is in! And it would be a crime if you didn't "Get Caught Reading" this May. So follow the clues to your favorite bookstore to pick up some great tips.

This month Harlequin Intrigue has the distinguished privilege of launching a *brand-new* Harlequin continuity series with three of our top authors. TRUEBLOOD, TEXAS is a story of family and fortitude set in the great Lone Star state. We are pleased to give you your first look into this compelling drama with *Someone's Baby* by Dani Sinclair. Look for books from B.J. Daniels and Joanna Wayne to follow in the months ahead. You won't want to miss even a single detail!

Your favorite feline detective is back in *Familiar Lullaby* by Caroline Burnes. This time, Familiar's ladylove Clotilde gets in on the action when a baby is left on a high-society doorstep. Join a feisty reporter and a sexy detective as they search for the solution and find true love in this FEAR FAMILIAR mystery.

Our TOP SECRET BABIES promotion concludes this month with *Conception Cover-Up* by Karen Lawton Barrett. See how far a father will go to protect his unborn child and the woman he loves. Finally, Carly Bishop takes you out West for a showdown under a blaze of bullets in *No One But You*, the last installment in her LOVERS UNDER COVER trilogy.

So treat yourself to all four. You won't be disappointed.

Sincerely,

Denise O'Sullivan
Associate Senior Editor
Harlequin Intrigue

SOMEONE'S BABY
DANI SINCLAIR

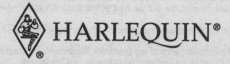

HARLEQUIN®

TORONTO • NEW YORK • LONDON
AMSTERDAM • PARIS • SYDNEY • HAMBURG
STOCKHOLM • ATHENS • TOKYO • MILAN • MADRID
PRAGUE • WARSAW • BUDAPEST • AUCKLAND

Special thanks and acknowledgment are given to Dani Sinclair for her contribution to the TRUEBLOOD, TEXAS series.

For Mary McGowan, who's done her best to keep me sane, a true friend in every way. And for Roger, Chip, Dan and Barb as always.

Special thanks to Linda Lou Mercer for allowing me to pump her knowledge of horses and guns. Any errors are mine.

ISBN 0-373-22613-6

SOMEONE'S BABY

ABOUT THE AUTHOR

An avid reader, Dani Sinclair didn't discover romance novels until her mother lent her one when she'd come for a visit. Dani's been hooked on the genre ever since. But she didn't take up writing seriously until her two sons were grown. Since the premier of *Mystery Baby* for Harlequin Intrigue in 1996, Dani's kept her computer busy. Her third novel, *Better Watch Out,* was a RITA Award finalist in 1998. Dani lives outside Washington, D.C., a place she's found to be a great source for both intrigue and humor!

You can write to her in care of the Harlequin Reader Service.

Books by Dani Sinclair

HARLEQUIN INTRIGUE
371—MYSTERY BABY
401—MAN WITHOUT A BADGE
448—BETTER WATCH OUT
481—MARRIED IN HASTE
507—THE MAN SHE MARRIED
539—FOR HIS DAUGHTER*
551—MY BABY, MY LOVE*
565—THE SILENT WITNESS*
589—THE SPECIALIST
602—BEST-KEPT SECRETS*
613—SOMEONE'S BABY

*Fools Point/Mystery Junction

All underlined places are fictitious.

CAST OF CHARACTERS

Jayne Bateman—She is anxious to make her mark as a private investigator, but she intended to be the hunter, not the hunted.

Cade McGovern—He is a loner and he likes it that way, but someone is bent on revenge and now he's stuck with a woman and her infant.

Heather—The two-day-old infant has no idea she's so popular.

"Hap" Ramirez—Cade's foreman has been with the ranch since his grandfather first started operations.

Maria D'Angelo—Cade's dead wife found a way to seek her revenge from the grave.

Luis D'Angelo—Cade's brother-in-law wants him to pay for his sister's death.

Zed Lithcolm—Cade's friend until Maria came between them.

Rio Cardonza—One of Cade's hired hands with no ax to grind, unless he was hired by someone else, as well.

Lily and Dylan Garrett—Jayne's mentor and her brother run the Finders Keepers Detective Agency out of San Antonio.

Diana Kincaid—Her kidnapping starts everything.

Thomas Kincaid—The Texas governor is out to destroy J. B. Crowe and his mob.

J. B. Crowe—He believes laws are meant to be broken.

Dear Reader,

I was really excited to be asked to be part of such
a wonderful continuity project. It's a bit daunting
to be the first book in such an extended series, but
a fun challenge. TRUEBLOOD, TEXAS involves many
exceptional category writers. Talented authors B.J. Daniels,
Joanna Wayne and I worked hard to make the Harlequin
Intrigue TRUEBLOOD, TEXAS prequel come alive for you.
We hope you'll go on to enjoy the rest of the series as
the tale of Lily and Dylan Garrett and the Finders
Keepers Detective Agency continues.

Happy reading!

Dani Sinclair

Chapter One

Being a freelance private investigator was exciting. Being a freelance private investigator was challenging.

Being a freelance private investigator was boring! Especially when you didn't have a case.

Jayne Bateman stopped her mental grumbling, set down her camera and reached for her soda. In the process, her purse slid to the car floor on the passenger's side, dumping its contents on the mat.

"Great. Just great." At least it hadn't been the soda.

So far her stakeout had been a total bust. Four days of watching in the hope that she might see something important. And all she'd seen so far was more people than she would have thought even lived in the county. What had seemed like a heaven-sent chance was now looking like an exercise in futility.

She hadn't meant to eavesdrop, but when her brother the cop had told her brother the judge that his tiny police force would have a problem staking out two locations every day for the next couple of weeks on the off chance a black-market baby ring might select Bitterwater for its next exchange, Jayne had been certain this was her big break.

Lily Garrett had told her all about the organized

baby-selling ring operating in Texas. The enviably tall, dynamic woman had sparked new interest in Jayne's chosen profession when they met at a seminar a week ago.

Lily Garrett was everything Jayne thought a private investigator should be. Intelligent, forceful, determined. She also happened to be strikingly attractive, yet people took her seriously. Lily and her brother Dylan had opened an investigative agency called Finders Keepers in Trueblood, Texas, just outside of San Antonio. She told Jayne their father had converted a big part of his two-story house for them to use as an office. And since Dylan had worked undercover for the police department for several years, his contacts gave them a huge edge.

Unfortunately, Dylan had been called back to work to assist the police in some sort of sting operation against the very mob that was selling black-market babies. Lily expected to be bogged down with work if she took on a couple more cases. She asked if Jayne would be interested in doing some freelance work for her from time to time.

Jayne was thrilled by the possibility. The Garretts were doing positive things with their agency by reuniting families. Jayne liked the sound of that and she liked Lily as well.

Jayne pushed aside a spill of pale-blond hair and surveyed the quiet shopping center over the tip of her straw. Few people ever took Jayne seriously. Okay, so she looked several years younger than her mature, twenty-four years—and she did slightly resemble the famous fashion doll because of her ash-blond hair and her petite stature. She was barely five feet tall if one counted high heels—and she always did. But what people overlooked was the fact that she'd grown up on a working ranch with three brothers. That meant she'd learned to compete at an early age.

The police academy hadn't worked out for her. Her brother the cop had made police work sound a lot more interesting than it actually was. Besides, there were entirely too many rules. Jayne never had been very good at taking orders. She'd left with no animosity and some knowledge and helpful skills.

In her mind, the next logical step was private investigative work where she could use her training and set her own rules. No way could she envision her life in some stuffy office or crowded city. And while she really enjoyed working with horses, her youngest brother already filled that slot in her family. He worked with their father training cutting horses. Jayne needed to carve out her own niche.

Unfortunately, if she didn't get a break soon, she'd be in real danger of starving to death first. She had quickly learned she was not cut out for spying on cheating husbands or running boring background checks, yet those were the only sorts of cases coming her way.

This baby-kidnapping ring, however, now that was something she could sink her teeth into. Lily had freely discussed what she knew about the mob-run black-market baby ring over lunch the day they met. Jayne had absorbed the information with rapt attention, wondering how any woman could sell off her own child. Jayne had overheard her brothers discussing that very subject in her father's barn a few nights ago.

Even Lily hadn't known that the police suspected the exchanges were made in small-town shopping centers. Nor had Lily known that a new exchange was about to go down any day now. Armed with this inside information, Jayne knew all she had to do was be in the

right place at the right time and her career would get
the boost it needed. Even her brothers would take her
seriously if she came up with a videotape of the
exchange and a list of license plates to go with it. The
police would then be able to nail everyone involved.

Lily Garrett might even offer her a permanent job.
Maybe Jayne could open a branch of Finders Keepers
right here in Bitterwater.

"Now if the baby-nappers would just cooperate…
preferably before I get arrested for loitering and talking
to myself."

But as morning slipped into late afternoon, their co-
operation was looking less and less likely. Too bad her
brother the judge hadn't known a time or the exact spot.
With Jayne's luck, her brother the cop would nail the
guys at Bitterwater's only other shopping center while
she was sitting here getting fat eating junk food in her
car.

Jayne was debating about going into the grocery store
to use the bathroom again when a blue sedan pulled
into the lot and parked several yards away from her car.
A middle-aged couple sat inside animatedly talking together for several minutes before they finally stepped
from the car. She had never seen either of them before.

Admittedly, Jayne didn't know every single person
who shopped here in Bitterwater, but she did know people who looked nervous and out of their element. The
woman was dressed in an expensive red sheath far more
appropriate for San Antonio. The same could be said
for her fancy hairstyle. Jayne brushed absently at her
own long, straight hair and continued her assessment.
The woman's dress was nice enough, but the color was
all wrong for her complexion. Even from this distance,
Jayne would take bets all that gold and glitter coming

from the chains and bracelets the woman wore wasn't costume jewelry. The woman was as out of place as a gelding in a breeding stall.

The man with her wore a tailored business suit that didn't come off a discount rack, either. He carried a shiny black briefcase that he gripped a little too tightly. His gaze darted about the parking area, nervously expectant.

And his tie was red. The red clashed with the different red shade of the woman's dress. Not significant surely, yet Jayne's brain wouldn't leave it alone.

Wouldn't that make a great identification signal? Nearly everyone owned something red, yet it was a color that would stand out without looking out of place. Jayne could almost hear the baby-nappers telling the buyers to come to the meeting wearing something red. The more she toyed with that thought the more she liked it. She watched the two of them closely, and dutifully wrote down their license plate number.

They were a mature couple, obviously not hurting for money based on their expensive car alone. And they made it clear they were waiting for someone. That didn't make them baby buyers. More than likely they were Realtors or something, here to use the small business center located a couple of doors down from the grocery store. Except they weren't paying the stores any attention at all. They scanned the parking lot as avidly as Jayne herself had been doing. She scrunched down a bit so they wouldn't notice her and tamped down a rising excitement.

She'd already been surprised by how many strangers actually used this shopping center. Especially at this hour of the afternoon. Still, these two people definitely stood out.

Jayne reached for her camera and snapped off a couple of quick shots. The couple suddenly came to attention. She lowered the camera and swept the parking lot to see what had captured their interest. A flame-red sedan drove sedately down the next aisle over. She'd never seen the car before nor either of the two men inside, but if she were going to typecast a couple of thugs, these guys would make her list. No necks, broad shoulders, low-sloping foreheads—perfect.

Jayne sank even lower in her seat. Since she wasn't tall to begin with, she didn't have to sink very far. Anticipation sent her heart dancing. What if this was it? What if she'd actually picked the right spot?

The red car pulled through a parking space and came to a stop only a few cars down from her. The two men stepped out, dressed in ill-fitting suits.

And they both wore red ties.

Her heart tried a triple jump in her chest. This had to be it. It had to be!

Raising her head cautiously, she watched them peruse the parking lot before striding toward the eager couple. Then she remembered she was supposed to be filming the exchange. The baby must still be inside the red car. From her angle, she could just barely make out a car seat jutting up in the rear seat closest to her.

This really *was* it! She'd done it! They were going to make the exchange right here in front of her!

Jayne reached for the video camera, shaking with excitement. When she turned back, guns had appeared in both beefy hands. The couple looked horrified. Jayne's own pulses leaped. The man was shaking his head, arguing, while the bigger of the two thug-types was staring at something beyond Jayne and to the left of her position.

Before she could twist around to follow that gaze, she saw the muzzle flash as his gun discharged. Something had gone horribly wrong.

The woman screamed. The man with her shoved her back toward their car. The other two men crouched down and fired again. Someone was shooting back and the car with the baby in it was right in the path of the bullets!

The couple fled toward their vehicle. Jayne dropped the video camera and opened her door. She had to get the baby to safety. If the men made it back to their car, God alone knew what would happen to the child. She could at least prevent them from taking it away.

Jayne flinched at the popping sound the guns made as she ran forward. Beside the car seat, the door was locked, but she glimpsed the infant sound asleep inside. It was so tiny it must have just been born. Any hesitation she had was gone. She must rescue the baby.

One of the thugs noticed her. He aimed his gun right at her. Jayne ducked and wrenched her shoulder opening the driver's side door. Keys dangled invitingly from the ignition. She seized the easy opportunity to get the baby out of the way and prevent the men from escaping at the same time. She slid inside and started the engine, but she had to stretch to reach the pedals with her toes. The driver was a lot taller than she was.

The big man lunged toward the car. Her fingers clicked on the automatic lock a split second before he grabbed the handle trying to get inside. He reached into the open window, and grabbed a handful of hair and the front of an earring before Jayne threw the car in gear. The man swore and brought up his gun. Using the tip of her shoes on the gas pedal, she pulled out of the parking space with a jerk. A shot whizzed right past her head and exited the driver's side window. Another man suddenly sprang out from between parked cars. He also aimed a gun at her.

The baby-nappers had brought backup!

Jayne hunched down behind the steering wheel and pushed down on the gas. The man fired right before he leaped out of her way. The windshield cracked as a hole appeared.

Quaking from head to toe, Jayne stayed as low as possible and tore out of the parking lot. The fiery red car nearly careened into an oncoming pickup truck. Avoiding the other vehicle forced her to turn right instead of left into town.

Her body trembled in reaction while her heart threatened to explode. She tore away from the scene with a squeal of tires. Shaken, but also giddy with her amazing success, she pushed the speed as fast as she dared. She had disrupted the exchange. She had saved the baby from being sold!

Unfortunately, she was speeding down the two-lane road away from town. She needed to get the car turned around so she could drive the baby into Bitterwater and the police station there. Her brother was going to have a cow!

Only, even scrunched down like this she could barely reach the pedals. She was going to have to stop for a minute and adjust the seat for her much shorter legs or she'd wreck.

Her elation was so high she was shaking. Wait until she walked into the police station with the baby in her arms. Her brother wouldn't be able to tease her about her choice of career anymore.

Jayne pulled off on the side of the road raising a cloud of dust. She fumbled for the lever that would let her pull the front seat close enough to the steering wheel that she could drive the car in relative comfort. Her left shoulder was beginning to actively hurt. She must have wrenched it badly. She resisted an urge to rub the sore spot. Instead, she cast a look over the back seat to make sure the baby was okay. The car seat faced away from her so she could barely make out the small infant, but it still appeared to be sleeping.

Confident now, and bubbling with excitement, she pulled back out onto the road ignoring her shoulder. There was a crossroad up ahead. She could turn around there. The scarred glass with the bullet hole in the center made it a little tricky to see, now that she was sitting up, but she could manage. She'd just rescued a baby amid a hail of bullets. She could do anything!

She glanced in the rearview mirror as she pulled out. A silver car was barreling up behind her.

Intuition, or even a premonition, had her pressing down on the gas pedal. Lots of people drove fast. It was practically a rule. It didn't have to mean a thing. But the car was gaining on her with single-minded purpose. She couldn't have said why she knew the driver was coming after her, but she didn't fight her desire to flee.

She came to the crossroad and took the turn too fast. She nearly lost control of the flame-red car. If there'd been another vehicle in the oncoming lane she would have crashed. The silver car followed closely behind her. Jayne didn't dare slow down now. She fed the car more gas. Her police training kicked in. With an effort, she steadied her breathing and concentrated on the skills she'd been taught about high-speed pursuits. Funny. She'd expected to use these skills pursuing the bad guys—not being pursued by them.

She whipped down secondary roads, going deeper

and deeper into unfamiliar territory. Her pursuer stayed right on her tail. His skills were obviously every bit as good as hers. Maybe better. He was gaining on her.

Without warning, she rounded a corner and came up on a horse trailer moving sedately along the narrow two-lane road. There was no time to slow down even if she'd wanted to. The shoulder abutted a gully. Her head pounded with fear as she pulled around him in the oncoming lane at eighty miles an hour. She barely squeezed back in before colliding head-on with an SUV heading in the opposite direction.

The sound of her heavy breathing filled the car. Her shoulder began to burn with surprising fire where she'd wrenched it. The baby began crying. Ahead was a major road. In her rearview mirror, she saw the silver car speed past the horse trailer. She'd gained ground, but not nearly enough. His car was faster. There was no choice. She whipped onto the new road amid honking horns and the squeal of brakes—and undoubtedly more than one curse.

She raced dangerously along the more heavily traveled, four-lane road, darting in and out among the cars, even using the shoulder to go around slower vehicles. All the while she prayed for a police car with flashing lights and a blaring siren. Instead, another quick glance in the mirror showed that the silver car was closing on her once again.

Impossible! There had to be a way to lose him.

Directly ahead was another cross street. An eighteen-wheeler hauling heavy bridge joists was in the right lane, lumbering along at a sedate fifty-five miles an hour. Jayne judged the distance. The timing would have to be exactly right or she'd kill both herself and the infant she was trying to protect. She knew she could make it. She also knew the silver car could not.

He was right behind her. She glimpsed his angry, set features in her mirror. With unnatural calm, she again measured the distance, saw there was no traffic on the secondary road, and cut directly in front of the semi at the last second. His horn blared a deep, furious warning as she sailed past and onto the side road, barely maintaining control over her car.

Instantly, Jayne dropped her speed. Something warm and wet ran down her left arm. She ignored it, bypassed the first side road she came to and kept going until she found a second one. The distances between roads became farther apart the longer she drove, but she repeated the process twice more before finding herself on a country lane in the middle of absolute nowhere.

Fences bordered the road indicating ranches or farms. Good. Her pursuer would never find her now. Even she didn't know where she was. All she had to do was keep driving until she—

A yellow light flashed on her dashboard. Her gaze flicked down and her heart began to pound all over again.

Low gas.

How could she be almost out of gas? What sort of criminals didn't fill their gas tanks?

Her gaze swept the surrounding countryside but saw nothing more than empty land. There wasn't a building or a silo to be seen, much less a gas station. Her left arm was not only hurting badly, but her fingers were starting to feel numb.

She glanced down and gasped. Her sleeve was stained a vivid bright red. Blood actually dripped from her wrist, discoloring the steering wheel and her pants.

Panic seized her as she realized she was bleeding profusely. She hadn't wrenched her shoulder. She'd been shot!

The knowledge opened the way for an instant rush of pain. She gasped again and bit her lip to keep from crying out. Now what? This wasn't a major road leading toward civilization and a doctor or hospital. And it had been a long while since she'd passed any other side roads.

Fear recharged her adrenaline. How badly was she hurt? She needed medical attention, but she couldn't stop now. While she may have lost the silver car for now, that driver was unlikely to give up. She'd take bets he was even now searching for her along these back roads. And this stupid red car stood out like a beacon.

Jayne prayed that she wasn't bleeding to death because there was no help for it. She ignored the pain and the blood and kept driving, looking for something familiar. Twice she saw dirt roads that may have led to ranches, but she was reluctant to try them for fear they wouldn't go anywhere at all. A line shack would be a death trap.

The baby's soft cries were increasing which only added another level of urgency.

"Easy little one. I'll get us out of this. Somehow."

If only she had her purse and her trusty cell phone. She could actually picture the small telephone lying on the floor of her car—along with the rest of the contents she'd spilled from her purse. Her daring rescue wasn't looking so daring anymore. Where the heck was a cop when you needed one!

The car began to sputter.

Either she pulled off the road or kept driving until

the car died right there in the middle of the street. A
drainage ditch ran alongside the road, barely leaving a
dirt shoulder here. Still, she couldn't see any other possibilities.

Jayne pulled over and turned off the key.

For a moment she just sat there. The infant's pitiful
cries reminded her that the child was her obligation
now. She ran her right hand up along the wet sleeve on
her left arm, probing for the source of the injury. Liquid
fire. She had to blink back tears.

Giving in to tears and just sitting there while she
waited for help was quite tempting, but she hadn't
passed another car in a long time. That meant she was
on her own.

Using her right hand, she reached across her body to
open the car door. Stepping out, she had to grip the
door a moment to keep from falling as a wave of dizziness washed over her.

Not good. Definitely not good. She swallowed hard
and forced her panic back. "You can do this!"

She let her left arm dangle uselessly and used her
right hand to open the back door where the baby's cries
helped put her own problems on hold.

"With lungs like that, at least I know you aren't
hurt."

But the baby was wet and probably hungry.

A large green-and-yellow bag sat on the seat beside
the infant. She needed two hands to unzip the bag. That
caused blood to flow alarmingly down her arm. She bit
down on her lip again to keep from crying out and
forced her attention to the bag. Inside was everything a
new mother might need. A package of six, already prepared bottles, a can of extra formula, a box of newborn
diapers, even a couple of tiny outfits.

Jayne didn't bother investigating the entire contents. It was enough to know she had the basics. Carefully, she pried her blouse away from her injured shoulder so she could inspect her injury. Blood flowed freely from an ugly raw wound that made her sick to look at. The bullet had torn away flesh as it skimmed across the top of her shoulder. If she wasn't mistaken, that was bone she glimpsed.

She tried not to be ill. "It's okay baby. The blood's not pumping or spurting like it would if the bullet had struck an artery." The brave words were of little consolation to her or the child. She was bleeding badly enough to be thoroughly frightened.

Using one of the diapers as a makeshift bandage, she covered the wound as best she could, applying pressure for a few minutes in an effort to slow the bleeding. But she couldn't just stand out here exposed. The baby-nappers would be searching for her. She needed to put distance between her and the silver car.

Pulling the car seat out was pure agony. She was tempted to leave the heavy plastic seat, but it would offer the baby some protection when she had to set the infant down so she could rest. Heck, she already felt woozy and who knew how far she would have to walk before she found help.

She finally got the baby and the car seat out of the car and removed the diaper bag. It struck her then, that it might be a good idea to hide the flame-red car as well. The color stood out like a beacon which would make it easy for the silver car's driver to spot.

She walked around to peer over the edge of the road. The drainage ditch was deep. Not deep enough to hide the car, but maybe deep enough that it wouldn't be noticed right away. After all, it would be dark in a few hours.

"Worth a shot," she muttered aloud.

There was enough gas left to get the engine started one more time. She put the car in neutral and aimed the tires at the ditch. A hard shove against the trunk was all that was required. The engine sputtered and died, but the car rolled far enough to slip over the edge. It made a satisfying crash as it tumbled down and flipped on its side.

The baby had begun crying in earnest. Jayne fought against adding her own cries. "I know you need to be changed and fed, but it's going to have to wait, okay? We're too exposed here."

She lifted the diaper bag, surprised by the weight. No way could she carry this on her wounded shoulder, but what choice did she have? She slipped the strap over her head so it would rest on her good shoulder and run across her chest. She bit back a moan when she moved her left arm to get it through the strap, but she managed. Then she lifted the carrier and set off down the road.

Every few yards she had to stop and rest. She was starting to think having the man in the silver car find her was preferable to this form of slow torture when she came across a side road that was slightly wider and better paved. Praying it led somewhere, she turned and started following the road.

Each step jarred her shoulder until all she could do was concentrate on putting one foot in front of the other. Jayne prayed for someone to find her because she wasn't sure how much farther she could go.

At some point, the infant stopped crying. She wanted to check on the baby, but was afraid to stop moving for fear she wouldn't be able to start again. She felt weak and sick to her stomach. Sweat beaded her forehead.

A sound up ahead made her lift her head. Her heart began racing. A gas station sign loomed like a beacon. A town! With renewed energy, she kept moving. Several small buildings squatted on the edge of the road leading into a small town. A combination feed-and-general store sat right beside the gas station. That meant people and telephones.

"We're going to make it, baby. Just hang on a little longer."

The baby didn't make a sound.

Jayne stumbled toward the nearest building which was the gas station. But as she drew close enough to call out, fear paralyzed her vocal cords. A car sat near one of the pumps. A silver car. The same silver car that had chased her from the shopping center.

Jayne came to a stop, swaying in the late-afternoon sun. Beside the car was a public phone. A man speaking into the instrument stood with his back to her.

There was nowhere to run, even if she had been capable of such a feat. A few yards away, a good-looking man was loading supplies into the back of a battered black pickup truck. Tall and lean, the rugged-looking cowboy lifted the heavy feed bags and slung them into the truck as if they weighed nothing at all. He shoved back the hat that sat low on his head and a lock of dark hair fell over his forehead.

She was tempted to call out to him, but fear kept her silent. The odds were too high that the man from the silver car would kill them both and then take off with the baby.

Without once looking in her direction, the cowboy pulled the tarp down over the last bag of feed. He didn't secure the load. Instead, he wheeled the long cart back inside the feed store.

Jayne called on the last bit of her strength. She skirted the gas station and headed for the pickup truck. Setting down the baby carrier, she tore the diaper bag over her head and thrust it into the bed of the truck as far back as she could manage. Ignoring the screaming pain that traveled up her neck and down her arm, as well as the fresh blood trickling past the makeshift bandage, she lifted the baby from the car seat and set her on a bag of feed. Awkwardly, she tossed the carrier under the tarp. The baby immediately awakened and began to whimper.

"Shh. Don't cry, baby. Not now."

Jayne climbed painfully into the back of the pickup truck. Every second she expected to hear a shout or feel a bullet in her back.

She pushed the carrier and the baby bag farther under the tarp toward the cab of the truck. Grabbing the crying infant, she slithered beneath the tarp with the child.

The truck bed was close to full, but she managed to make a place for herself and the baby up near the cab between two heavy bags of feed. If the man got off the phone and started in this direction, the crying would draw attention. Frantically, she opened the baby bag and withdrew a bottle of formula. Terrified they would be discovered at any moment, it seemed to take forever before she got the bottle ready and into the infant's wailing mouth.

The baby immediately stopped crying and began to suck avidly. Jayne sank back, totally drained, the infant cradled against her bad side.

Moments later, a man's low curse choked her with

dread. The truck's owner threw back the edge of the tarp.

Her terror escalated as she waited for him to discover her. But instead, he continued cursing as he pitched several more items inside and drew the tarp back down.

"Afternoon," another man's voice called out near her head.

The cowboy grunted and began tying off his tarp.

"I was wondering if you've seen a woman and a baby in a red sedan," the voice asked.

The man from the silver car was practically next to the spot where she lay. She didn't breathe, praying the baby's sucking noises weren't audible through the tarp.

"Nope."

Her inadvertent rescuer had a deep soothing rumble of a voice. He managed to convey disdain and disinterest in that single syllable.

"My wife and I had a stupid fight," the man from the silver car continued. "She ran off with the baby before I could apologize. I'm afraid she may do something foolish and hurt herself."

Jayne continued to hold her breath. The baby's slurping sounded so loud over the pounding of her heart she was certain the two men would hear.

"Haven't seen any red cars with or without a woman driver. Now if you'll excuse me..."

The cab door creaked open.

"Okay. Sure. Thanks, anyhow."

Jayne didn't release her breath until the engine started and the truck began pulling away. She'd done it! They were safe. As soon as the truck came to a stop again, she'd ask the man to call the police.

Her head fell back in exhaustion. She only hoped she didn't bleed to death before the truck stopped.

Chapter Two

Cade McGovern pulled off his dusty Stetson and set it beside him on the passenger seat. He chomped down on the toothpick in his mouth and chewed thoughtfully. "Dumb bastard. He'd be smarter to let her go," he muttered.

In his mirror, Cade watched the other man staring after him, before turning to walk back to his silver car. Cade could have been nicer, he admitted to himself. It wasn't that poor bastard's fault that Cade was out of sorts with himself and the world at large.

He'd jammed his thumb good on that cart when he started loading. Besides, Cade wasn't fond of strangers and he hated coming into town. Technically, Darwin Crossing wasn't enough of a town to make most maps, but it was as close to so-called civilization as he wanted to get. He could live just fine without other people and their problems. Especially some jerk old enough to know better than to saddle himself with a runaway wife.

At least Cade's former wife, Bonita, had been smart enough not to get pregnant before she ran off, he thought grimly.

Thinking of Bonita caused him to bite down harder on the toothpick. How come all the paths in his head led to thinking about her lately? She was the last person he wanted to think about. No man liked to remember past mistakes, and Cade had never made a bigger one.

He'd been old enough to know better, yet her dark flashing eyes, sultry smile and lush beauty had nailed him like a deer caught in headlights. His grandfather had tried to warn him about women and ranching, but he hadn't listened. Family history alone should have warned him.

It was funny, too, because Cade had been a loner by choice, ever since he could remember. Even when he was riding the rodeo circuit he'd kept to himself. Of course, in retrospect he realized that had been the draw for Bonita. She'd seen him as a challenge. And a winner, of course. Bonita wouldn't have given him the time of day if he hadn't been successful.

Cade cursed. She was haunting him from her grave.

No doubt because of the recent acts of sabotage on his ranch. He hadn't gone out of his way to make enemies, so he could think of only one person who might have a reason to be causing him these petty problems. Luís D'Angelo. Bonita's younger brother, was the only man alive who hated him that much. Luís blamed Cade for his sister's death. He didn't seem to find it significant that she'd died in a car crash with a man who wasn't her husband. Luís was convinced Cade had been abusive and chased her away.

Cade could have told him how far off the mark that was. He could have told Luís several truths about his sainted sister, but the kid had only been sixteen when she died and in a moment of misplaced gallantry, Cade hadn't wanted to totally disillusion the boy. So now the kid was out to destroy Cade and his ranch. And he didn't seem to care who got hurt in the process.

Two of Cade's men had been injured in the stampede someone had deliberately started while they were trying to move the herd yesterday. That was how Cade got saddled with coming into town today. With his banged-up elbow, Rio couldn't lift the heavier supplies they needed and Sven had bruised a couple of ribs. Cade was only thankful that had been the worst of it.

Only plain dumb luck had kept anyone from getting hurt in the fire in the grain silo last week. Fortunately, Hap had spotted the smoke right away and the fire was put out before much damage was done. But the way these attacks were escalating, it was only a matter of time before someone got seriously hurt.

Cade's foreman, Hap Ramirez, had wanted to call the sheriff in the beginning, right after the fences were cut and several girths were slit. Cade had found himself reluctant to send the law after his brother-in-law because of his age. But now, it looked like the kid was going to give him no choice in the matter.

This was a busy time on a working ranch. A time when a man didn't need to be out hunting some fool kid hell-bent on a vendetta to avenge a cussed woman who hadn't been worth it in the first place. With a sigh, Cade turned on the radio to drown out his thoughts.

He decided in town not to go straight back to the main house. The way things were going it had occurred to him that it might be a good idea to pick up some extra supplies and take them out to the old line shack. A backup location might come in handy in case the kid decided to torch the house next. Cade and his men couldn't be everywhere at once. The Circle M was a large spread in the middle of nowhere. Normally, that suited Cade just fine.

He debated about calling Hap on the radio and letting

him know about the change in plans, but the dour older man already had his hands full right now, especially since he was down three men with Cade gone, too. They needed to get the rest of the strays rounded up and the herd moved this week. Of course, Hap could run the Circle M by himself after all these years. He'd been foreman for Cade's grandfather since forever. It had come as a shock to all of them when the old man succumbed to a bout of influenza and died unexpectedly last year.

Known for being a crusty old curmudgeon, Otis McGovern had nevertheless taken in his only grandchild after the deaths of Cade's own parents. Unfortunately, not before Cade had spent several years being shuffled from one foster home to another. Otis and his son hadn't spoken in years, so it was some time before Otis learned what had transpired.

By the time Otis convinced authorities to let him have guardianship, Cade had a chip on his shoulder big enough to be visible a mile away. Otis ignored the chip. Being a cowboy from the old school, and a loner himself who liked it that way, he took Cade's chip to be a matter of course. He took in his bewildered, angry grandson and taught him the only skill he knew. Ranching.

The two of them had butted heads like a pair of bulls after a rodeo clown. Neither knew how to back down. Yet somewhere along the line, Cade came to realize that he loved ranching and the land as much as his grandfather did. Still, as big as the ranch was, there could only be one person in charge. Cade finally walked out after a heated argument over some breeding stock and headed for the rodeo circuit. He'd been determined to win himself a stake that would let him buy a place of his own up in Colorado. He hadn't wanted anything half as ambitious as the Circle M, just a small spread he could run himself.

Oddly enough, that pleased his grandfather. On Cade's infrequent visits home, they got on better than they ever had when they'd lived together.

Cade let his thoughts roam the past until the line shack finally came into view. For a moment, he sat in his truck just drinking in the rugged beauty of the landscape. Jagged cliffs formed a backdrop for the shack. They fed the stream that ran to a small pond down below. The Circle M boasted some fabulous grazing land as well as several thick draws that were a haven for deer and other wildlife. The peace of this land never failed to move him. Several times Cade had thought this particular spot would have made a better location for the main house than the one his grandfather had selected all those years ago.

Maybe he'd unload everything and spend the night here. The idea had definite appeal. He must have had some subconscious thoughts along this line because he'd thrown his gear into the truck before he headed into town.

Cade pulled around in a semicircle in front of the shack to facilitate unloading. He turned off the engine, swung down from the cab, and settled his hat back on his head, low over his eyes. He tossed the mutilated toothpick into a thicket of brush and started to undo the tarp. A small mewing sound of distress made him pause. A kitten? What would a kitten be doing way out here? He looked around, hoping he hadn't hit some animal when he pulled in.

Nothing moved anywhere nearby. Cade cocked his

head, listening closely. The sound seemed to be coming from inside the bed of his truck.

He hurriedly unlashed the tarp and started pulling it back. Blood stained the nearest sack. Some poor little critter had obviously hurt itself and climbed in the back of his truck to nurse its wounds. And from the trail of bloodstains, the wound was probably going to prove fatal on a small animal. With a new sense of urgency, he yanked back the tarp, snagging it on something. Cade barely noticed.

There was no kitten in the back of his truck. Instead, shock held him still when he revealed a woman's dainty foot, half in and half out of a small, badly scuffed loafer. A length of shapely leg was also revealed due to a rucked-up pant leg. Several nasty scratches ran along that leg, but nothing serious enough to account for the blood on the feed sacks. He ignored the pounding of his heart, unhooked the snagged tarp and stripped it all the way back.

The body and the face that went with the leg were definitely worth a second look. But from the blood that had soaked one side of her sheer blouse, the woman could be dead already.

For a moment, cold panic swept him. Clutched protectively against her chest was a tiny infant, its red face screwed up in distress. Its tragic cries sounded a bit like a kitten in distress.

He reached over the woman to lift the infant. Cade had never in his life held a live human baby this small, though he'd helped bring plenty of animals into the world. This little guy couldn't be more than a couple of days old at most, he guessed. He checked it over quickly, looking for the source of the blood. There was no outward sign of injury and based on the amount of blood, there would have been. The blood must have come from the mother.

Cade swore under his breath. The woman never moved.

Instantly, his mind pictured the jerk outside the feed store. The man had said he was worried about his wife. Cradling the crying infant in one arm, he studied the woman. More of a girl, really, with a long spill of blond hair that partly covered her face. She didn't move. With a sense of fatality, he reached out to feel for a pulse.

She had one! A fairly steady one at that. She was still very much alive.

One hand holding the baby, he gently, carefully, rolled the woman on her back to look for the source of the blood. Under her blouse something bulky lay against her shoulder. He worked the top two buttons of her blouse free and pulled out one of the baby's disposable diapers.

"I'm afraid she may do something foolish and hurt herself," the man had said. But Cade knew a bullet wound when he saw one. The bullet had chewed a path right across the top of her shoulder, tearing away the material of her blouse.

He couldn't think of a single person who'd ever tried to commit suicide by shooting himself there. He examined the ugly raw wound. Unless he missed his guess, she'd been shot from the back, not the front.

Even if he was mistaken, an accidental shooting victim wouldn't climb in the back of a stranger's truck to hide. The bastard had shot her!

Cade growled, torn by conflicting emotions. On the one hand, he could understand all too well the anger a woman could raise in a man. On the other, there was no valid excuse for violence against a woman. Especially one who had to be half the bastard's size—and age, judging by appearances. How could the bastard shoot her when there was an innocent little baby involved?

Cade muttered a curse. The last thing he wanted was to become embroiled in someone's domestic problems. The woman had left him no choice. He'd become involved the moment she'd climbed into the back of his pickup truck and sought refuge.

He'd lose hours turning the truck around and taking her back to Darwin Crossing. Besides, it was a trip she might or might not survive, given her condition. When he thought of the jolting ride she must have endured back here under the hot tarp, he winced. No wonder she was unconscious.

The blood had stopped flowing, but she definitely needed medical attention. Only, the nearest doctor was almost an hour away. No doubt her jerk husband had discovered the doctor's location as well. He'd probably be there waiting for her to show up.

The baby began to wail in earnest. A movement in the truck drew his gaze back to the woman. Even unconscious, she reached blindly for her child. Something inside Cade loosened at that sign of protective love.

A small bottle lay beside her. She'd obviously been trying to feed the tyke before she passed out. He frowned over the fact that she wasn't nursing, but maybe she couldn't. It probably wasn't safe for her to do so with that bastard coming after her.

He reached for the bottle and stuck the nipple in the little guy's mouth. Greedily, the baby began to suckle. Dark-blue eyes opened and gazed up at him with such trust that Cade knew he was lost. A child needed its mother. He knew that better than most.

And in this case, the mother needed a protector. Looking at the tiny infant he knew he'd just been elected. There was no way he was driving them back into harm's way until he knew what the situation really was.

Since she was breathing okay on her own, and not bleeding anymore, he decided to deal with the infant first. The crying had been more than he could stand. He wanted to make absolutely sure the baby wasn't hurt.

His medical skills were limited, but any good rancher knew enough first aid to deal with emergencies. What Cade didn't know was what to do with a human infant. Give him a cow or a horse or even some poor kitten— no problem. But God help him, he'd never even contemplated changing a diaper before. Yet the kid was soaked. It couldn't be good for the little guy. Holding the baby and bottle awkwardly in one hand, he reached for a large, soft bag that had become jammed between the cab of the truck and some sort of baby carrier.

The yellow-and-green bag hadn't been there when he first began loading the truck so he guessed it was hers. There were blood smears on it, as well. No doubt he'd need both the contents of the bag and the carrier that doubled as a seat.

The dark, dusty interior of the unpainted building was less than welcoming. Cade frowned. It was a line shack, for crying out loud. There was one window and one door. This was a place where a couple of men could throw down their gear and sack out on the bunk beds, protected from inclement weather. He took mental inventory. It housed a cookstove, a few dishes, some implements, the bunk beds, a wobbly table and four chairs. There was a lean-to out back with a couple of stalls for horses and some oil lanterns for light. And thankfully, a pump to provide water. Beyond that, there were no amenities.

Well, it was what it was. The shack would do until he could determine how badly she was hurt.

Awkwardly, he set down the carrier and placed the baby inside. The minute he removed the nipple, the infant screwed up its face and began to wail.

"Okay, look. Just hold on for a minute. I've got to see to your mother. You can finish eating in a second."

The baby was in no mood to be placated by mere words. He was hungry and he was letting Cade know it. He howled at the top of his tiny lungs.

"Certainly can't be anything seriously wrong with you if you can scream like that." Cade wasted a few minutes grabbing his kit from the front seat of the truck and spreading his sleeping bag over the lumpy mattress. Then he returned to the truck for the woman.

She moaned softly when he lifted her, but those sweepingly thick dark eyelashes only fluttered against her pale cheeks without raising. She was incredibly slender. Why, she didn't weigh much at all.

Long, pale hair spilled like ribbons of satin against his toughened skin. He tried to pretend that he didn't notice how good she smelled or how pretty she was. Her graceful neck draped limply over his arm. Like her kid, she was a tiny bit of a thing. Small boned, delicately shaped, she had an upturned little nose and soft, nicely shaped lips.

And a bullet hole in her shoulder.

Cade toughened his heart and his thoughts. He carried her inside and laid her down on his open sleeping bag. She was pretty, but young. Much too young for an old man like him. In fact, too young for the jerk claiming to be her husband. No wedding ring, either, he noticed. In fact, no rings at all.

Since carrying her inside hadn't started the bleeding up again nor roused her, Cade turned his attention back to the screaming infant. He was afraid the little guy would hurt himself crying that hard.

The baby quieted instantly as soon as the nipple returned to his mouth. Cade let him drink for several minutes before pulling the bottle back. He had to get the supplies inside before it got dark. Junior was not happy.

"Okay, fella, hold your horses. I'll be right back."

He off-loaded the food supplies first. Then he dug out the first-aid kit and a couple of jugs of fresh water, removed the spare blankets and added the two new shirts he'd bought himself today. The young woman would need something to put on once he cut off her fancy shirt, and these were all he had to offer beyond the change of clothing in his bedroll.

The baby had really worked himself into a state by the time Cade hauled all the stuff inside. He dropped his hat on a chair and turned back to the infant.

"Shh. Hush. It's okay. The feed bags can wait. I'll get them later." He withdrew another bottle from the contents of the bag and stuck the nipple back in the baby's mouth with one hand and tried to unwrap the kid with the other hand.

"We've got to get you out of this wet stuff. You stink worse than the outhouse, kid. You'll get a rash or something sitting around in it like this."

What the heck was he doing playing nanny to some baby? He didn't know anything about kids. Especially one as small as this. He'd probably hurt him with his big clumsy hands. Look how tiny his fingers were! How could something this small make so much noise?

"You're awfully loud, you know that, tiger?" The baby ignored his commentary to suck down the formula.

"Man, you were thirsty. Guess I shouldn't be surprised. It must have been hot as Hades under that tarp. But you're going to get a stomachache drinking like that."

In the end, he waited for the baby to finish the bottle. The kid instantly began to whimper again wanting more.

"Hang on. I'll see what I can do as soon as I get you changed, okay?"

Obviously it was not okay based on the noise and the way the baby began to flail his arms and legs. Cade stripped away the wet garments. A gauze pad covered his stomach. For a second, his heart stopped. Had the infant been hurt as well? He peeled back the pad carefully and discovered the stump of the umbilical cord.

Cade swore. "Sorry, kid. But that looks nasty." There was dried blood around the withering navel. Was it supposed to look like that? Should he be doing something for it?

"Why couldn't you have been a kitten?"

First, he'd better get the wet diaper off. Paying close attention to the way the diaper fastened, he removed it.

"You're a she!"

Why that surprised him, he couldn't have said, but the infant quieted at his exclamation. She stared up at him with wide, trusting eyes.

"Oh, yeah, you're definitely a female. Don't be batting those baby blues at me, kid. You're like every other woman I've ever met, you don't like being wet or dirty, do you? Must be something you're all born with. Now hold still while I give this diapering business a try. How the heck is this supposed to work? You're a lot smaller than these diapers, kid… No… Hold still. Don't kick your legs like that… Will you hold still?"

It was like trying to pin a wet octopus. Her arms and legs thrashed and she began crying again, probably wanting more milk. Eventually he got her wiped off and the dry diaper in place—after a fashion.

"It ain't pretty, kid, but it should do the job."

He found rubbing alcohol in his kit and dabbed a little on the cord where it had been bleeding. The baby objected.

"Sorry, little girl, but you'll get an infection or something." He covered the area with some antibacterial cream and a small bit of gauze.

After digging through the bag, he came up with a second outfit and finally won the battle of getting her into it. Then he reached for another bottle of formula.

"Mouthy little thing, aren't you? You want what you want when you want it." But he found an unaccustomed smile curving his lips as he watched her drink. She was beautiful. Her eyes stared complacently up at him, then closed peacefully as he rocked her gently in his arms.

"You're going to grow up to be a heartbreaker, you know that? You'll lead some dumb male on a merry chase, won't you, little one?"

Running the back of a knuckle over her soft skin, he marveled at her tiny countenance. There was something almost soothing holding her like this. Wisps of light-colored hair and a small pointy chin were her only real distinguishable features. He glanced over at the mother to see if her chin was pointy, too, and found himself being observed by a pair of light-blue eyes.

"So, you're awake. How do you feel?" Unnerved to be caught off guard that way, the words came out sharper than he'd intended.

The woman's mouth parted dryly. The tip of her tongue licked at her chapped lips and he realized the baby wasn't the only one who was thirsty. She tried to sit up and her face contorted in obvious pain. "Is…the baby okay?"

"Your daughter is fine. She was just wet and hungry. I'll get you some water and have a look at your shoulder in a minute. She's already polished off a bottle and a half and she's nearly asleep."

The cabin was growing dark. He needed to get the rest of the supplies inside and arrange some light so he could see before it grew too dark. A fire wouldn't be amiss, either. He'd need to make dinner and he desperately wanted a cup of coffee.

The baby's frantic sucking had slowed right along with its breathing. He took a chance and set the infant back in her carrier. With a contented sigh, she seemed to settle back, peacefully asleep. Cade reached for a lantern and used a few seconds to fire up the wick.

"Let me get a fire started and put some water on to boil, okay?"

The woman's eyes had closed again. She didn't answer. He walked over and laid a hand on her forehead. A little warm. Was she running a fever? He hoped not. His first-aid kit wasn't as up-to-date as it should have been. She lifted her eyelids with obvious effort to peer up at him.

"Here. Let's try a little water." He found a cup, wiped it out with the inside of his clean handkerchief and offered her water from one of the jugs he'd brought inside. Like her daughter, she drank thirstily as he held her silky head. Damn, but she had nice hair, even if some of it was matted with dried blood. Her eyes closed and he laid her back down.

"Stay with me, okay?"

"'kay," she whispered, but she didn't open her eyes again.

Cade frowned. This wasn't a good sign. How much blood had she lost? The wound might become infected. Bringing her inside had been a really bad idea. He should have taken her straight back to town or over to the doc's place.

"Listen. Can you hear me?"

"Yes," she replied without opening her eyes.

"I'm going outside to the truck. I'm going to radio Hap to send us some help. It's going to take awhile, but I'll get you to a doctor as quick as I can, okay? Miss? Hey. Can you hear me?"

He touched her cheek lightly, but she didn't move. Her chest rose and fell in steady rhythm. She'd fallen asleep.

Or into a coma.

That thought scared him with gut-clenching intensity. As he squatted beside her, the sound of his truck engine coming to life was like an unexpected thunderclap. Cade leaped to his feet. In three short strides he was at the door.

"Hey! Hey hold it! Come back here!"

Someone was stealing his truck!

Cade raced after the vehicle as it barreled away down the rutted path that served as a road. He shouted to no avail. The bastard had no intention of stopping. While Cade hadn't gotten a clear look at the driver, he didn't need to. It had to be his brother-in-law, Luís.

But how had the kid known where he was? How had anyone known where he was?

An icy finger of fear raised the hair on the back of his head.

What if he was wrong? What if that hadn't been Luís?

In the deepening twilight, Cade controlled a moment of panic. He forced himself to think. The line shack was a long way from the road. Hell, it was a long way from anything. How had Luís gotten here?

Cade surveyed the landscape surrounding the shack. There was no sign of another vehicle or a horse but the kid couldn't have walked in. A drifter? There was a draw out behind the cabin to the east a ways, and of course the hills behind the shack. It was possible that a drifter had been camping nearby and seized the moment.

It was also possible that the drifter hadn't been alone.

That thought stopped him cold. The isolation of the line shack was complete. Without that truck he had no means of communication or escape. Cade cursed his stupidity and the bastard who had driven off. His options had just vanished, leaving him stranded with a badly wounded woman and an infant.

Another chilling possibility worked its way forward. What if the woman's husband had followed him here? A remote chance, but barely possible. He hadn't really paid any attention to others on the road once he left town.

If it had been the husband, the bastard would have had to leave that little silver car of his out near the road. That meant he walked in, which meant his car wasn't far away.

If it had been the husband.

Cade couldn't leave the woman and the baby alone to check out that theory or any of the others. This was a perfect place for an ambush. Once he was out of sight all the bastard had to do was ditch the truck and circle back to the clearing.

Cade swore viciously. Every possibility he could think of presented potential danger. His rifle was inside his truck. The only weapon he had with him was a .38. He was pretty sure it only held three or four rounds.

Cade headed back inside. He lit a second oil lamp and dug his gun out of his gear. The feel of the heavy metal was reassuring. At least he wasn't totally defenseless.

His pulse hummed with tension as he walked back outside and checked the wood box. Supplies were on the low side, but adequate for tonight. The real blessing was that he'd unloaded the important supplies before the bastard stole the truck. He had food, bottled water, blankets and his gun. What he didn't have was a radio, transportation, more than one box of diapers or a lot of spare formula for the baby.

He hoped the woman could breast-feed soon or they were going to find out how the infant liked powdered milk. Cade primed the pump and let the water run until most of the brown discoloration was replaced by clear water. He filled a couple of pans with the water and lit the wood-burning stove. After stacking more wood inside, he dragged the table full of supplies over against the front door. At least no one could walk in on them without warning. Finally, he was able to turn his attention to the woman.

Girl, he corrected himself harshly, looking down at her relaxed face in the soft yellow light of the lantern. She couldn't be more than sixteen or seventeen. Much too young to be married, let alone have a child. If he had that jerk bastard from the crossing here right now, he'd happily beat the man to a bloody pulp.

As far as Cade could see, the girl hadn't moved. He grabbed the first-aid kit and braced himself for the delicate operation of removing her blouse.

He'd intended to cut the material away from the wound, but given the new situation, he might need to cut his spare shirts into diapers. There was only the one box of diapers tucked inside the bag she'd carried. Who knew how long those would last? He'd have to remove her blouse carefully and try to wash the blood out so she could wear it again.

Fresh blood matted the thin material, adhering it to her like a second skin. Cade frowned. How much blood had she lost? If that bullet had nicked the bone or an artery they were going to be in serious trouble.

If only she wasn't so pretty. Why couldn't she have been some fat old hag? He was feeling like a dirty old man for even noticing this one was female.

Taking a deep breath, he undid her buttons quickly. A lacy, white bra that fastened in the front was revealed. He had no intention of touching that! And he carefully averted his eyes from the sight of her small, high round breasts nicely filling the flimsy material. Cade cursed beneath his breath.

This was going to be harder than he'd thought. She lay like a rag doll as he lifted her slight weight and untucked the blouse from her slacks, slipping the white material off her good arm. She moaned softly as he laid her back down.

"Hey. Wake up. It would be a big help if you'd open your eyes and give me a hand here."

No such luck. Her skin definitely felt warm and dry

to the touch. Not a good sign. He'd take bets she was running a fever. He prayed the wound hadn't gotten infected.

Water boiled on the stove. He let it go and rolled her to one side so he could ease the blouse away from her injured shoulder.

She was as delicate and fragile as a small bird. In back, the material of the blouse had crusted against the wound. He tried to ease it free gently, but the scab broke, starting a fresh trickle of blood.

With a muttered oath, he wadded her sleeve and pressed it against the wound, all the while thinking how badly he wanted five minutes alone with the bastard who'd shot her. At least the bullet hadn't gone into the shoulder, but it had taken out a lot of tissue as it plowed a groove through her skin alongside the bra strap.

He had no business playing doctor with a wound this serious. He should have driven her back into town as soon as he found her, husband or no husband. But it was no use thinking what he should have done. The important thing was to do the right thing for her now.

He pressed against the wound until the bleeding stopped, then he stood, whipped off the bandanna from around his neck and put it into the pan of boiling water. All the while he cursed himself for a fool.

He made himself wait five full minutes before he fished the bandanna out of the water with a fork and held it over the small sink until it cooled enough so he could wring it out.

Gently, he began washing away the dried blood from around her wound. She shifted restlessly. He had to hold her still so she didn't roll onto her back.

"Easy. I'm cleaning away the blood. Hold still, okay?"

She was worse than her daughter. Cade couldn't tell if she heard him or not, but the sound of his voice seemed to soothe her, so he continued talking as he worked.

"This needs stitches, little girl. I've got some thread and if you were a man, I might be tempted." But she was definitely no man and he couldn't bring himself to stick a needle into her soft, white skin.

"I'm going to pour some disinfectant into the wound. It's gonna sting, but we need to keep it from getting infected." He wondered if she heard or understood anything he was saying. "I'll have to use butterfly bandages to try to pull the skin together. I've got tape and gauze so I'll wrap it tightly. That should hold you until I can get you to a doctor."

God only knew how long that would be.

There was no way to lower the strap of the bra without jarring the wound. She wasn't going to like it, but he used his knife to cut the strap before he set some fresh water boiling on the stove and stoked the fire. He couldn't stall forever. He was going to have to get this over with. He debated between the iodine or the rubbing alcohol. But the alcohol would disinfect the wound and he could put some of the antibacterial cream on it afterward. If this didn't wake her, nothing would.

He poured a small amount of rubbing alcohol directly into the wound. She cried out and opened her eyes, instantly shutting them again tightly.

"What are you doing?" she demanded in a raw voice as he mopped up the dripping excess.

"We have to prevent infection."

"I'll take my chances with the germs." Watery blue eyes glared up at him. "Get that stuff away from me."

"Don't worry, I'm done. I need to put some cream on the wound."

"No." Her lips set in mutinous lines of determination.

"Look, you're in no position to be giving me any grief. Hold still or you'll start it bleeding again."

"No. I— Ow! That hurts!"

"All done."

She blinked back tears as he blotted her chest lightly with his handkerchief.

"How would you like me to do that to you?" she growled, brushing away a tear.

He tried not to feel bad or guilty over causing her more pain. "I'm not injured."

"I can fix that."

Cade's lips twisted in a smile in spite of himself. The girl had spunk. "Let me put on a bandage."

"Forget it. Let me die in peace."

"You aren't gonna die."

"I am if you keep helping me."

His lips twitched. Her voice might be weak, but she had spunk. Her grit came as a complete surprise. He'd expected buckets of tears. She had to be in considerable pain.

"It was an antibacterial cream."

"I know what it was and my shoulder hurts like the devil. Will you just take me to a doctor?"

"I'd love to, but we have a problem."

Her tired eyes opened again. "What problem?"

"Someone stole my truck."

"What are you talking about? Where are we?"

"We're at a line shack on my ranch."

"Well, call someone!"

"Happy to oblige, but the radio is in the truck."

"Then use your cell phone."

"I don't have one."

"Everyone has a cell phone these days."

Cade shook his head. "I'm not real fond of modern technology."

"Yeah. I could tell from your archaic idea of medicine. What are you doing?"

"Tryin' to put a butterfly bandage over the bullet hole. And it would be a whole lot easier if you'd hold still and cooperate."

"I don't trust you."

Offended, he pursed his lips. Ungrateful little witch. "Well, get over it. Right now, I'm all you've got."

She glared at him, but held still while he applied the bandages and began to wrap her shoulder. Suddenly, her eyes grew wide.

"You took off my blouse!"

Embarrassed, he didn't meet her eyes. "Tough to tend your wound with it on. I had to cut the strap off your bra as well."

"You didn't," she gasped.

"'Fraid so, but you can't wear it over that shoulder anyhow. And your blouse won't be good for much even after I wash it out. Don't worry. You're perfectly safe with me."

"You're gay?"

Indignant, he glared at her. "Of course not!"

"Then why should I believe I'm safe with you?"

"Because my taste doesn't run to mouthy juveniles with tiny babies and a gun-toting husband," he snapped in reply. "I take it he was the one who shot you?"

Her eyes widened and her mouth opened, but she swallowed back what she started to say and looked at him strangely. "Who are you?"

"Cade McGovern. Who are you?"

"Jayne."

He waited but she didn't offer a last name. The baby stirred behind him as he finished wrapping the tape around her shoulder.

"Well, Jayne. I hope you're prepared to breast-feed because your daughter will soon polish off those bottles you were traveling with and I don't imagine powdered milk is going to make a good substitute."

Chapter Three

Jayne thought frantically past the pain in her shoulder. This sexy man with the incredible voice thought she was the mother of the baby. She hadn't even known it was a girl.

Caution curbed her first impulse to tell him everything. She didn't know him or anything about him. But watching him with the infant had brought a lump to her throat. For such a large man, he handled the tiny baby with a gentle touch. He hadn't seemed awkward, just a bit unsure which endeared him to her. He was obviously a good person.

Though he'd hurt her, he'd been nothing but kind trying to fix her shoulder. It was probably insane, but she trusted him. The only problem was, the kidnappers had already proved they would stop at nothing. Was it fair to involve him any further in this mess?

"Who stole your truck?"

His eyes darkened and a hardness set in around his mouth. "Good question. I don't like any of the answers including the possibility that your husband may be outside right now with my rifle trying to figure out the best way to get in here and finish the job he started."

Fear returned with a vengeance. In her mind, she

clearly pictured the man standing in the parking lot aiming the gun at the car she stole.

"You think he followed us here?" She swallowed past her dry throat.

"It's not a possibility I'm willing to rule out."

"We've got to get out of here!"

She tried to sit up but he held her in place easily with one hand. She was so weak the effort nearly drained her and the motion jarred her shoulder alarmingly. She could have wept from the searing pain.

"We've got no place to go," he said soothingly.

"But—"

"I'm not completely unarmed," he told her. The flick of his hand sent her eyes to his waistband where the handle of a gun protruded. "He'll have to go through me to get to you."

That braked the fear and reached into her muddled mind with a whole host of confusing sentiments. He was going to protect her?

"You don't even know me."

"No, ma'am, I don't. And if you'd had the decency to pick someone else's truck to hide in, I'd have been a whole lot happier. But you didn't, so I'm stuck with the situation."

Jayne blinked in surprise at this grumpy discourse. "And here I was thinking you were a nice person."

"Whatever gave you that impression?" he growled.

"I have no idea," she snapped weakly. "I suppose I could have just stood there and let him shoot me, but I assure you, he probably would have shot you, too. He's even nastier than you are and he's not apt to leave witnesses. He just wants the baby."

"Good."

"What?"

"If she's what he wants it gives us an advantage."

New fear washed over her. "I am not giving him the baby!"

"Of course not, but it means he won't start shooting indiscriminately into the cabin."

Jayne tried to hide a shudder. She closed her eyes and attempted to think. Her uncooperative brain was sluggish with pain and fear and exhaustion.

"Why would he take your truck? That doesn't make sense. He could have walked in the door and shot us both when you weren't expecting him. He doesn't need your rifle. He's already got a gun."

Silence filled the cabin.

"Good point," the man called Cade finally said thoughtfully.

"And why don't we have anywhere to go?" she asked, opening her eyes again. Cade wasn't looking at her. He was staring at the wall apparently deep in thought.

"This is a line shack," he said after a long pause. "We put them in places that are far from the main house. After a day roping cattle or riding fence it's a roof over your head instead of a bedroll on the ground. Especially during bad weather."

She knew that. "So walking for help isn't an option?"

"Not at the moment." He pulled a toothpick from his pocket and stuck it in his mouth. Grimly, he stood and began packing supplies away. "You can breast-feed, can't you?" he asked again.

"No!"

He suddenly eyed her with an expression of disdain. Did he believe she felt such a natural process was beneath her?

"There's milk in the diaper bag."

"She already drank two of the six bottles. They're really little bottles."

"There's an unopened can of formula. We'll have to mix up more formula when we run out."

He turned and began rummaging through the bag. He pulled out the can and gave her an acerbic look. "This won't last forever. Then what?"

"I don't know! Are we going to be stuck here forever?" She tried to sit up, but her shoulder hurt and the action made her feel weak and dizzy. Her stomach lurched appallingly. She tried to cover her helplessness with a glare. "You can wipe that expression right off your face. I'd feed her if I could, but it isn't possible."

Her head began to ache in tandem with the burning throbbing of her shoulder. Jayne closed her eyes against the pain and vowed not to be ill. "I don't know what to do," she said trying not to panic. "I can't seem to think right now."

"Okay," he said more kindly. "I've got powdered milk. I can add it to the formula to stretch it out a ways if we need to. It may not be great, but it should get us through until help arrives."

She opened one eye and immediately closed it again. She was very tired and it was cold in the cabin.

"So help will arrive?" she asked.

"Let me worry about that. When's the last time you ate?"

She thought about the bag of cheese curls and the diet soda she'd been eating in her car right before everything went crazy. Her stomach tightened alarmingly.

"I'm not hungry."

"I'll fix us something while you rest."

"The baby—"

"Will be just fine. She's still sleeping. What's her name?"

Name? Of course he'd expect her to have a name. He thought this was her baby.

"Heather. I call her Heather." Her mother's name was the first one to pop into her head.

"Yeah?"

She squinted carefully and found him scrutinizing the sleeping infant.

"I guess I can see that. It's soft. Sort of pretty."

"My mother will be glad you approve."

Cade glanced at her. "Why? Did she name the kid?"

"No. It's her name."

"Oh. Are you cold?"

"What gave it away, the shivering or the chattering of my teeth?"

He shook his head and walked over to the table. "Here." He came back with two blankets which he spread over her. But when his hand reached out to brush the hair from her forehead she tried to draw back.

"What are you doing?"

"Hold still, I want to see if your head is warm. We don't want you getting a fever."

"And just how are you going to prevent that?"

He didn't bother to respond. His hand was large and rough. The hand of a workingman. Yet his touch was somehow reassuring against her skin. She didn't want to be drawn to this surly cowboy, but she was. At the moment, he represented safety and security.

"Well?" she asked as he pulled back.

"Can't tell."

"That's helpful."

He tried to mask his irritation by turning away. "Rest

while I get the supplies organized and make us something to eat.''

She didn't bother arguing with him. The way her stomach felt at the moment, food was the last thing it wanted to deal with. She had a bad feeling those cheese curls were looking for a quick way out.

She tried to focus on Cade, but she found watching him unnerving. Especially after he took off his jacket and draped it over the back of a chair. He moved like a feral cat, she decided. Muscles rippled beneath the denim work shirt. There were no wasted motions other than the toothpick he chewed on. She wanted to ask him if he'd just given up smoking or something, but any more conversation seemed like an awful lot of effort.

She was cold despite the blankets. Much too cold considering the air temperature. She probably was running a slight fever, but she was too tired to tell him so. Why did her shoulder have to hurt so badly? She closed her eyes and gritted her teeth, content to listen to him moving about the room.

Unbelievably, she fell into a light doze, waking partially when she heard the baby crying. She should get up and change the little thing, but she couldn't quite force her eyes open. Her shoulder was on fire and her head throbbed like anything. She wanted nothing more than to cry right along with the baby.

The cries grew louder, more demanding.

Cade's voice began to speak. The baby quieted at the sound. Jayne didn't blame her. Cade had a fabulous voice. Deep. Soothing.

She tried to force her eyes open. She should get up. The baby wasn't Cade's responsibility. But it had stopped crying. Maybe she'd just lie there a couple more minutes. Then she'd get up and do her part to help.

"JAYNE. Jayne!"

The voice was insistent. Demanding. Sexy.

She didn't want to leave this incredible dream. Hard, callused hands had been running through her hair, stroking her tenderly. Those lips had been inches away. He had such a sensual mouth.

"Jayne, wake up. Come on. Open your eyes."

The man in the dream faded to black. Cade's voice was no longer sexy.

Opening her eyes took a lot of effort, but she wanted to see his features. She peered at him through slits. Dark-gray eyes loomed over her in concern. She had to blink several times to bring Cade's blurry face into focus.

"That's it. Wake up, little one."

"I'm petite not little," she corrected. Her mouth was so dry it seemed filled with cotton.

The lines around his eyes crinkled. "Wake up petite one doesn't have the same ring to it," he said.

Inexplicably, she wanted to smile, but her lips wouldn't make the effort. "Tired."

"I know you're tired, but you have to eat something."

"No." She promptly shut her eyes again. Her shoulder burned with pain and she ached in places she normally never thought about. She sensed him moving away and tried to call back the velvet warmth of sleep, and that wonderfully erotic dream that had slipped away. What would Cade's lips feel like pressed against her own?

The scent of food tickled her nose. It mingled with

the smell of wood smoke. Her stomach growled. Maybe she was hungry after all. But getting up was far too much work. It would hurt.

Wasn't getting shot bad enough? Topping it with at least a ten-mile hike carrying the baby and gear had nearly done her in. The unbearable truck ride had depleted her completely.

She had no reserves left. Zip, zero, none. Her back and hips felt black and blue. She'd bet she had bruises all the way down her spine.

"Try this."

Cade cupped the back of her head and lifted her slightly. This should have been like her dream, only the movement made her arm hurt like crazy. She wanted to tell him so, but he pressed something against her lips. Liquid, but warm. She didn't care. She was so thirsty. Taking a cautious sip, she allowed the broth to slide down her throat. It received an enthusiastic reception. She placed her good hand over his to steady the cup and drank greedily.

"Easy. Don't choke, there's bits of meat and vegetables in there."

She opened her eyes all the way. His face was inches from her own. All the tiny lines at the corners of his eyes were visible. How old was he? There was a small scar over one eyebrow and another one near his left cheek. Jayne resisted an urge to touch them.

There was something sensual in the way his hand threaded through her hair, cupping her head like this.

Why did she keep thinking thoughts like that?

"Want some more?"

"Please."

Approval shone in his dark-gray eyes. He lowered her with tender care and she followed his path to the

stove. His jeans were old, fitting snugly enough to outline muscles that had come from hours of hard work.
Cade had a nice butt. Heck, he had a nice everything.
He must have women falling all over themselves to get
close to him.

What was wrong with her? Must be the fever. She'd
never noticed a man's body before in her life. She had
entirely too many males hitting on her as it was, and
she'd learned early on that men only wanted one thing
from petite blondes.

"Think you can sit up?" Cade asked as he returned.

"Not without a lot of pain."

He made an amused sound low in his throat. "Let's
give it a try anyhow. I'm going to support you until you
can lean back against the wall here. Okay?"

"Couldn't I just lie here and die in peace?"

"No."

He placed his arms around her carefully and lifted.
She was intensely aware that her breasts were covered
in nothing but her thin bra, and one side of that no
longer gave any support. Her breasts pressed against the
material of his shirt. If he noticed, he gave no sign.

She should have been embarrassed, but that required
more energy than she could summon. On the other
hand, she was so busy being aware of him and the stubble on his firm, square jaw that she forgot to cry out in
pain until she was already upright and he was moving
away from her.

She yanked up a blanket self-consciously and tried to
keep her eyes open. Cade seemed to be unaware that
she was even female. He pulled over a rickety chair to
use as a makeshift table. Asleep in her carrier, the baby
sat on another chair closer to the fire.

"Are you right-handed?" Cade asked.

"Yes."

"Good. Eat what you can, and holler if you need help."

There was a spoon for the stew, but he'd put it in a mug so she had the option to drink it instead. There was also a can of cola and an empty cup.

"Aren't you going to eat?"

"Already did."

"Oh."

He walked back across the room and began doing something in the small sink. Since he had his back to her, she gathered he wasn't interested in making conversation. She wasn't used to men ignoring her. But she wasn't used to getting shot, either. She was a mess. Obviously, he resented her and why shouldn't he? Look at the trouble she'd caused him.

She ate the stew hungrily at first, then drank some of the cola. She really was thirsty—and warm. No doubt about it, she was running a slight fever. That sobering thought sent butterflies of fear scurrying around inside her. If she got an infection and they truly were stranded, she could die.

Jayne made an effort to finish her small meal but pain and fatigue soon took over. Staying upright became an effort—one she didn't think she could continue to maintain.

As if summoned, Cade appeared beside her. "More?"

"No. Thanks. It was good, but—"

"You want to lie down. Swallow these first."

She looked at the two white pills in his hand. "What are they?"

"Don't look so suspicious. They're aspirin. You have a fever."

"Noticed that, did you?"

He smiled with his eyes and she put the pills in her mouth, swallowing the tepid water he held out to her. Her eyes were closed before she even got horizontal again. She felt him adjust the blankets. Her breath caught when he brushed back several strands of hair from her face. The action felt tender and personal. She wanted to see his expression but her eyelids wouldn't cooperate. Hovering on the brink of sleep, she knew he watched her for several long seconds before he moved away.

Cade McGovern was an enigma. A lot of cowboys had come through her father's ranch looking at horses. Many were loners or drifters and men of few words, but none had been as good-looking as Cade. Nor could she picture one of them diapering a baby with such tender care.

Who was this man?

Her sleep proved fitful. Several times she heard the baby cry and Cade's mellow voice as he spoke quietly to the infant. She knew she should help, but she couldn't make her body cooperate. Her system went from sweats to chills and back again. More than once, she heard herself moan out loud. Each time she felt Cade's hands on her, soothing her with his voice and cool wet cloths. Twice he had her swallow more water and aspirins.

She tried to cooperate. Even apologized for being a burden, but she was too weak to do anything but lie there and suffer while her shoulder ached even when she didn't move.

It was her bladder that finally pulled her from sleep. Something heavy pinned her to the bed. Fear roused her mind to full consciousness as she realized she wasn't

alone on the cot. Heart pounding, she found Cade Mc-
Govern curled beside her, one arm flung over her waist,
holding her in place. For a moment she didn't move as
panic swept her. But he was asleep and fully dressed
from what she could see. In sleep, his features had softened the harsh set to his jaw. This was a young man's
face. A face an angel might covet.

Her body relaxed as adrenaline seeped from her system. The idea of this big strong cowboy as an angel
nearly made her smile. Maybe she should still feel
threatened finding him in bed with her like this, but
logic told her he was just tired. Now that she thought
about it, she dredged up a dim memory of him actually
getting into bed with her to try to stop the chills that
had been setting her teeth to chattering.

Having a man in her bed was a novel experience.
One that would have worried her under other condi-
tions. Right now, her bladder reminded her that there
was a reason she was now awake. The problem was,
Cade looked so peaceful she hated to disturb him. Judging by the light in the cabin, morning wasn't far off.
She tried to lift his arm away. It might as well have
been a tree trunk. His hand snugged her closer in sleep
and began to stroke her side like a lover. Despite his
jeans and her own slacks, she felt a bulge that was instantly recognizable.

Jayne tensed. Cade opened his eyes.

"What's the matter?"

Several responses popped to mind, but she settled on
the simple truth. "I have to go to the bathroom."

"Oh." His hand came away from her body and he
rolled off the narrow cot and came to his feet in one
graceful motion. She tried not to stare at that portion of
his anatomy that was in her direct line of sight.

It would seem his body was proportional.

"There's a pail over there in the corner."

That snapped her gaze back to his face. "You're kidding."

"I'll turn my back."

"I'll go outside!"

"No, you won't."

He didn't waste words or motions. From the hard set to his features, this issue wasn't up for debate. She thought about what he'd told her happened to his truck and decided he was right. Going outside alone in the dark was a bad idea. But a pail in the corner?

"Where's the baby?"

He tipped his head. "Over there. In the car seat. She's sleeping peacefully." He reached out and felt Jayne's forehead before she could move. "At least your fever broke. Go use the pail."

Her gaze swept the cabin. It landed on her blouse, draped over a chair close to the fire. "You washed it!"

"It's got a hole in it and not all the blood came out, but I figured you'd need it come morning. You might be better off with one of the new shirts I picked up in town."

His thoughtfulness left her speechless. A blue denim shirt draped one of the other chairs.

Jayne got off the bed slowly. She was as wobbly as a foal trying to stand for the first time. Cade watched her closely which might have added to her embarrassment if she hadn't known he was ready to steady her if she began to fall. He'd returned the table to its original position and she decided she could lean on that if she needed support.

She surprised both of them by laying a hand along his scratchy cheek before he could pull back.

"I was right the first time. You're a good man, Cade McGovern. If I had to get myself into this fix, I'm glad it was your truck I crawled into."

His discomfort was obvious. She walked over to the table, so weak it was amazing she didn't totter. She pulled on her torn shirt to act as a robe for the rest of the night, then lifted a roll of toilet paper that sat there, and headed for the corner. If Cade could give her his brand-new shirt and tend to her and the baby, the least she could do was not make a fuss over a pail in the corner.

The process was awkward given how weak and light-headed she felt, but she got the job done and managed to admire Cade's back in the process. Solid, dependable and sexy. What more could a woman ask for?

"Thanks," she said walking unsteadily over to where he stood looking at the infant.

"Didn't like my shirt, huh?"

"I'm saving it for the morning. This is already ruined, so I might as well sleep in it."

He nodded. "Want something to eat or drink?" he asked.

"Water. But you don't have to wait on me."

He didn't waste words. He filled a mug from a plastic gallon container of water. Their fingers brushed as he held the cup out to her. He must have felt the same jolt of awareness she did because he pulled back so fast she almost dropped the mug. He waited without saying anything while she drained the contents and handed him back the empty cup.

Getting into the narrow cot once more, she slid over against the wall as far as she could and waited. He went over to the sink and rinsed the cup. Then he stoked the fire. When he pulled up a chair and straddled it backward she ran out of patience.

"Come back to bed!"

"I'm fine."

"You're exhausted."

"Don't worry about me. Get some sleep. It'll be light soon."

Stubborn man.

"You know, being a hero is hard work. But being a martyr is plain stupid."

His jaw went slack. "What?"

"I'm in no condition to ravish you. Sitting in a chair for the rest of the night is pretty darn stupid, wouldn't you say?"

"I'd say you don't have any sense whatsoever. Do you make a habit of inviting strange men into your bed?"

Her cheeks heated at the deliberate way he framed the question, but she refused to lower her eyes. "No, you're the first."

He looked pointedly at the bunk over her head. "Cabbage patch?" he asked archly.

"Back seat of a car."

"Yeah? Proves my point. You shouldn't have gotten into a car with a man old enough to be your father in the first place."

Jayne realized he thought she'd meant she got pregnant in the back seat of a car. And she remembered that he thought the man chasing her was her husband. His assumptions made her angry. "He was hardly old enough to be my father."

Cade snorted.

She started to explain and stopped. Her head was

starting to throb again right along with her shoulder. She was too tired to argue with him.

"This is a stupid conversation. Will you please come back to bed and lie down?"

"No."

"Fine. Just remember, most martyrs die a horrible death. And if something happens to you, I don't even know which direction I should head to find help. But you suit yourself. You can take the top bunk. But, hey, if you'd rather sit on a hard wood chair to prove what a man you are, do enjoy yourself."

She closed her eyes, but not before she saw something that could have been amused admiration in his expression. She was nearly asleep when she felt him slip in beside her. Her heart soared right along with her pulses.

Baiting him had been one thing. The reality was something else altogether. She'd made a mistake. She'd thought she could ignore him. What had she been thinking? Despite her fatigue and her injury, she was all too aware of every inch of the rock-solid man at her side. He was a large man. All over. She should never have insisted he share the bed.

Cade immediately rolled on his side so his back was to her. "Sleep. It's gonna be a long day," he mumbled as if reading her thoughts.

Yeah? Well it was going to be a long few hours until morning, too. But surprisingly, she did sleep, only slightly disturbed when he got up to tend to the crying baby. The low murmur of his voice was a soothing cocoon that seemed to work on her as well as the infant.

When her eyes finally opened for good, dust motes danced in a room awash in light. Cade sat next to the table holding the baby in his large, capable arms, talking seriously to the infant. On the table was a partially drunk bottle.

"I know you don't like it. I don't blame you. But we're fresh out of the premixed stuff and your mama said she can't breast-feed. This is the best we can do. You have to drink it until we can get out of here." He touched the baby's cheek tenderly with a long blunt finger.

Jayne's heart melted at the sight. He'd be a wonderful father. Were all the women around here complete idiots? Somebody should have put their brand on this cowboy a long time ago.

He offered the nipple to the tiny mouth once more and crooned encouragement as the baby began to drink. Obviously, she was not happy with the taste or quality of the milk, but she did drink it.

Jayne lay quietly watching, enthralled by the sight of Cade and the infant. Until this minute, she'd never given much thought to being a mother herself. She was young. She had her whole life ahead of her. On the other hand, she loved working with the kids who came to her parents' ranch. Having a child of her own would be a wonderful thing.

Not until he set the empty bottle back down on the table did Cade look in her direction.

"How's the shoulder?"

No "Good morning." No "So, you're awake." Cade cut right to the chase. Her tranquility vanished with his abruptness. Well, she could be terse, too. "I'll live. Did you burp her?"

"Burp her?"

He stared as if she'd said something foreign.

"Yeah. You know? Put her against your shoulder and pat her back until she burps? It prevents gas bubbles."

Cade scowled, but he put the baby on his shoulder and began patting her back. He seemed surprised when she cut loose with a loud belch.

"She doesn't like the powdered stuff," he muttered.

Jayne sat up carefully and waited for the room to steady. Not good. If anything she felt weaker than she had last night. She swung her legs over the edge of the bed, trying to pretend her body wasn't screaming in protest.

"I need to change the dressing on your shoulder."

She shook her head. "It's fine."

"You were running a fever last night and your color's high again this morning. I need to check the shoulder."

From his tone, arguing would get her nowhere.

She used the pail in the corner while he fussed with the baby. She was dizzy and weak and sore. Her shoulder hurt more than anything ever had in her life, but she was determined to be just as stoic as Cade.

"Scrambled eggs okay?" he asked as she collapsed onto the chair that he'd vacated by the table.

"I'm not hungry." That response seemed more restrained than telling him that the thought of food repulsed her to the point of gagging.

Cade eyed her grimly. He secured the baby in her car seat and strode toward Jayne. A lion with easy prey. "Let's have a look at that shoulder."

"Let's not and say we did."

Ignoring her, he reached out and began helping her off with her torn shirt. Yesterday when she'd been more unconscious than awake it had been bad enough, but today she was fully aware of how sheer her bra was and the fact that one side dipped revealingly. This was an extremely sexy man she didn't know at all who'd

already seen her breast fully exposed and could undoubtedly see her nipples through the thin lace.

"You don't—"

"Hold still." He had her shoulder beneath his hand
before she could pull back. "This is going to hurt."

She drew in a strained breath as he began to peel
away the binding. All thought of sex faded as he exposed the wound.

Cade muttered a curse that filled her with dread.

"Is it infected?"

"Nothing a little penicillin wouldn't cure."

She looked at the wound and felt sick and scared to
her toes. "Do we have any penicillin?"

"Back at the ranch."

"Think we could send for it?" she asked weakly,
hoping he couldn't hear the fear behind her words.

He didn't answer which only made it worse. His expression scared her silly. When he crossed to put a pan
of water on the stove she looked more closely at the
wound. It was ugly, deep, raw and puckered. Even she
could see it was becoming infected.

"What are you doing?"

"I'm going to open the cut a little and try to draw
some of the infection out with hot water."

"I don't think so. That sounds painful."

"You can handle it."

His matter-of-fact words left her with nothing to say.

"I'll have to open the scab. It will hurt a little," he
told her. "And this cloth will be hot. I'm going to press
it against the wound. We'll do it a couple of times, then
we'll pour some rubbing alcohol in there."

"Sounds like fun," she said grimly.

"Better than having gangrene set in."

She couldn't argue with that.

"Here. Swallow these."

She swallowed down the aspirins and ordered her stomach not to reject them. It was a near battle, but she won.

"Ready?" he asked.

"Not if I live to be a hundred. So go ahead."

She couldn't stop the indrawn hiss or the tears that poured down her cheeks, but she refused to cry out. The pain made her dizzy and sick. She refused to pass out either. She'd show this man that she could be as tough as she needed to be, despite the fact that his form of torture seemed to last endless hours. When he was done, she sagged limply against the chair while tears continued to flood her face.

"Here. Drink this."

The kindness in his voice sent more tears over the edge. "Will it be okay?"

He stroked her hair. She could almost close her eyes and believe it was a lover's caress. He blotted the tears on her cheeks with tender kindness.

"You're a survivor, just like your daughter."

That opened her eyes. "Look, there's something you'd better know—"

"Shh!"

Jayne didn't even breathe as he reached for his gun.

"Get over by the baby," he said so softly she had to strain to hear him. "There's someone outside."

Chapter Four

Cade reached for his gun as Jayne grabbed the shirt he'd left out for her and struggled into it. He flattened himself beside the lone window at the front of the cabin. He could barely see out past the accumulated dirt.

Part of him felt surreal, like a movie actor playing a role, while the other part tamped down real fear. He'd heard a horse whicker. Someone was definitely out there. But who? None of his men should be over this way unless Hap had gotten worried and sent out a search party. It was early for that, but possible.

More likely, it was the bastard who'd left them stranded here in the first place. But what had been the point? Jayne's comment about her husband had made inarguable sense. That left Luís or a drifter as prime candidates for grand theft auto. Cade didn't like either possibility.

Noise carried clearly from the shelter behind the shack. Someone was stabling a horse? Whoever was outside was making no effort to keep quiet. Cade scowled. They got occasional drifters on the Circle M. But being a drifter didn't make the person any less dangerous. Just the opposite.

Cade darted a glance toward Jayne. She was no

longer standing beside the bed. Lines of pain bracketed her mouth, but she'd taken the metal frying pan from the hook near the woodstove. As he watched, she walked unsteadily up behind the door, holding the pan firmly in her good hand. He didn't know whether to mentally applaud her bravery or curse her foolishness. What did she think she was going to do with a frying pan?

He shook his head at her and motioned her back. She lifted her chin and the pan, determination in every line of her body. From outside, someone began to whistle a popular country-and-western tune, slightly off-key. There was no time left to argue as the door handle turned. Cade aimed for a body shot and waited while the door swung open.

Zedekiah Lithcolm sauntered two steps into the room and came to an abrupt halt. The whistle broke off with a surprised woof of air. He held his traveling bag in one hand, saddlebags and a rifle in the other.

Of all the possibilities that had come to mind, Zed hadn't even been on Cade's list.

"Hell," Zed drawled. "I knew you wouldn't want to see me again, but I didn't expect you'd shoot me on sight."

Cade didn't lower the gun. Mixed feelings tore through him. Zed had been his friend once. One of the few he'd made on the circuit. Zed rode the bulls, Cade roped the steers. The two of them had often shared drinks and even rooms together to cut costs.

They'd also shared Cade's wife, effectively ending their friendship.

"What are you doing here, Zed?" The words came out more evenly than Cade had any right to expect.

"Lookin' for a job."

Cade narrowed his eyes. "At a line shack?"

"No, I was plannin' to rest here for the day and ride down to the ranch tomorrow. Lafferty stumbled this morning after I broke camp. He didn't come up lame, but he's pretty tuckered so when I spotted the shack I decided we could both use a day of rest."

It had the ring of truth. But then, Zed had always been glib and quick with his words.

"Say, if you're not going to shoot me out of hand, could you lower the gun and let me drop my gear? My arms are gettin' tired."

Cade's gaze flew to Jayne. She still stood behind Zed, unnoticed. And she still gripped the frying pan as she watched Cade for cues. Taking a deep breath and releasing it through his nose, he gave her a half nod and lowered the gun. Zed spun toward her quickly.

"Whoa! Hello, there. Looks like I'm interruptin' big time." His infectious grin spread as he directed all his charm at Jayne. "But if you were plannin' to brain me with that thing, darlin' you'd need a ladder. You're a little bit of a thing, aren't you?"

Standing there in Cade's too big shirt that was buttoned all wrong with her hair long and wild about her head, she looked like she'd been making love. Cade felt his groin and his anger tighten at the same time while Zed's grin spread.

"Actually, I had a much lower target in mind," she said mock sweetly. "Once you take out the kneecap and the groin, the brain's easy to reach—assuming it can be found."

Cade felt a sense of intense satisfaction at her words and her tone. Jayne wasn't buying into Zed's notorious charm. Zed whirled back to him with a startled expression. Cade let his lips curl up at the corners.

"I think she's serious," Zed said.

"Believe it," Jayne agreed.

"What the hell's goin' on here, Cade?"

Cade shoved the gun back in his waistband, but he left his hand resting on it as he indicated a chair with a nod. "Have a seat. You can drop your gear right there, but set the rifle down nice and easy. I want to see your hands the entire time."

"Have you lost your mind? What's going on?"

"Do it, Zed."

All humor was gone. Zed knew him well enough to know he wasn't kidding. With exaggerated motions, Zed set the rifle on the floor, then set his gear beside it.

"Take a seat," Cade ordered.

Questions spilled from Zed's eyes. He sat stiffly, his gaze swinging between Cade and Jayne. There were some interesting lines of strain around his mouth and eyes that hadn't been there the last time Cade had seen him. Zed had always been a big man like Cade—tall, but rangy. Only now Zed was downright gaunt. Those lines were lines of pain, Cade reflected. He wondered what had happened to the other man, but he wasn't taking chances.

"Jayne, get the rifle and bring it over here. Where's your .45?" he asked Zed.

"In my saddlebag."

The baby chose that moment to announce her presence with a loud wail. Zed's mouth dropped as he darted a look at the bunk bed. Then he swung an assessing look at Jayne.

"You robbin' cradles now, Cade?"

Cade ignored the question. Jayne skirted Zed's chair and picked up the rifle.

"Where were you camped yesterday?"

"Hell. What sort of trouble you in, buddy?"

Weakly, Jayne kicked the saddlebag farther away from where Zed sat. But she lifted the rifle with the ease of someone who knew exactly what to do with it if she had to. The woman managed to continually surprise him.

"It's loaded," she announced.

"Of course it's loaded! Wouldn't be much point in carryin' it empty now, would there?"

"Let me see it," Cade said.

"I know a loaded gun when I hold one," she told him.

"But do you know if it's the one from my truck?"

"Oh." She held it out to him, looking embarrassed.

"Your truck? Why would I have— What in thunder is goin' on here, Cade? I feel like I'm in the middle of a grade B western."

Hadn't Cade felt exactly the same way? He glanced down and saw the rifle wasn't his. He shook his head without touching the weapon and focused his attention on Zed. There was a time he would have trusted the other man with his life.

He just shouldn't have trusted Zed with his wife.

"You'd better see to Heather," he told Jayne.

The baby's cries were escalating. Jayne gave Cade a disgruntled look and Zed a wide berth as she headed back to the bunk beds with the rifle. At least now she was armed. After watching her with the frying pan, Cade had no doubt she'd use the rifle if she felt threatened. She probably would have done some damage with the pan as well, he decided. Cade rocked back on his heels.

"Someone stole my truck late yesterday afternoon. Know anything about it?"

"How would I know anything about that? I don't even understand what's going on around here. I made camp up in the hills out back last night. Late."

"How late?"

"I wasn't lookin' at my watch, but it was almost dark when I found a spot. If I'd known the shack was here, I'd've come down even in the dark."

"Where's your truck?"

"I sold it and the trailer."

Cade stared in astonishment. "Why would you do a thing like that? They were practically new."

"I needed the money. It's a long story. You want to tell me what's goin' on here first?"

"No."

Zed glanced at Jayne. She held the baby against her good shoulder and observed the two men warily. Pain shadowed her eyes.

Zed gave a tuneless whistle. "O-kay. I had a bad run of luck a few months ago. Got hung up during a competition. Damn bull dragged me clear around the ring more than once before they got me free. That was one mad bull. He gored me, then stomped me pretty good. Surprised you didn't hear about it."

"I don't keep up with the circuit anymore."

Zed shrugged. "By the time I paid the medical bills—"

"You had insurance."

"*Had* being the operative word. Seems I missed a couple a payments and they dropped me. What you see is what I got left. I kept Lafferty instead of the truck because he can run on grass instead of gas."

"So what are you doing here?"

"I told ya. Lookin' for work."

That surprised Cade more than Zed's tale of injuries.

Bull riders were always getting hurt. But the last time he'd seen Zed, Cade had knocked the other man halfway across the room. They hadn't spoken since.

"Why come here?"

Zed shrugged. "I didn't have anywhere else to go."

Cade stared at the man he'd once called a friend and tried to decide if Zed was telling the truth. Like him, Zed had been a loner. He never talked about his past any more than Cade did. Cade didn't really know much about Zed. But what would be the point in lying? Bonita was dead. Cade didn't have anything else Zed might be interested in. Still, he couldn't bring himself to completely trust the bull rider. Not anymore. And Cade didn't like coincidence. Especially when Zed just happened to arrive here at this particular time.

Jayne watched quietly as she rocked the baby in her arms. She looked young and vulnerable and in pain. The bright-pink glow to her cheeks told its own story.

"You only have Lafferty?" Cade asked.

"And my gear, such as it is."

The quarter horse was high-strung for a gelding. He might let Cade ride double on him, but the odds of him carrying a crying baby in addition were too low to consider. Cade couldn't take a chance on riding Jayne and Heather out of here on Lafferty. But if he didn't get some antibiotics into Jayne soon she was going to end up in serious trouble.

Jayne laid the baby down and reached for a diaper. Fool woman didn't know when to ask for help.

"I'll change her," he said.

"I can do it."

"You'll start the shoulder bleeding again. I'll take care of her." He turned to Zed. "Were your injuries serious enough to require antibiotics?"

Zed grunted an affirmative. "Oh, yeah."

"Got any with you? That you can spare?"

Zed looked at Jayne. "Sure."

"Get them."

The room went silent for the beat of a heart. Even the baby seemed to be listening.

"All right."

Zed stood slowly. Jayne reached for the rifle sitting beside her, but Cade shook his head.

"He said he had a .45 in his saddlebags," she reminded him.

"It's okay. I don't think Zed plans to shoot us."

"Hell," Zed muttered.

Cade didn't sit down beside the baby until Zed finished rifling through his bag and came up with a prescription bottle that rattled nicely.

"I've got more'n I thought. Looks like a couple of days' worth here. You aren't allergic to anything are you?" he asked Jayne.

"Yeah, people who shoot guns at me. But I don't have any medical allergies."

Zed's mouth dropped open, his handsome face looking almost comical. "You were shot?"

"Her husband shot her in the back," Cade said quickly. "The bullet tore across the top of her shoulder. The wound's starting to get infected. I planned to walk out and go for help today. Now I won't have to."

It was a question and a challenge. Zed realized it immediately. He nodded. "No, you won't. I can have Lafferty saddled again in five minutes. Here, ma'am. You might want to take two of these tablets to start. You want to get a large dose in your system to begin with."

Cade inclined his head in agreement and turned his

attention to the baby. Heather continued her protest of the messy diaper.

Amazingly, Jayne didn't argue about the pills. That chewed on Cade. With her, silence wasn't exactly the norm. He wanted to check her forehead to see how hot she felt, but he suspected she wouldn't appreciate it under the current circumstances. She took the bottle of tablets from Zed cautiously, read it, thanked him and walked over to the jug of water.

"I'll pour it for you," Zed offered.

"I can manage."

"I don't doubt it for a minute, ma'am, but my mama raised me to be courteous and friendly."

Cade blew out a puff of air and fastened the tape on the diaper.

"Thank you," Jayne said.

"If you don't mind my askin', what are you puttin' on the wound?"

"I cleaned it and used some antibacterial cream," Cade told him.

"Let's not forget the rubbing alcohol," Jayne interjected. "I haven't."

His lips curved up. That was more like it. "And most of my rubbing alcohol," he added for Zed.

"Then I'll leave you my medical kit. I've got some clean bandages and other things you might be able to use."

Cade inclined his head in thanks.

"I've also got some pain medication left. Looks to me like the lady needs it more'n me."

It was plain she wanted to refuse, and telling that she didn't.

"Thank you," Jayne said when he handed her a second bottle with a couple of tablets inside. "What about a cell phone?" she asked.

"Sorry."

"What is it with you people? I thought everyone had a cell phone these days."

"I'd need to have someone I wanted to call first."

Jayne swallowed down the water and the pills, swaying slightly. Cade started to rise, but saw Zed was watching her closely. He turned and their gazes locked in mutual concern.

"I'll saddle Lafferty,"

"Okay," Cade agreed. "And Zed?"

The other man stopped, his hand resting on the door handle.

"Tell Hap I just hired you on. We'll see how it goes."

For a moment, Zed didn't say anything. They looked at one another, no longer friends, but no longer enemies, either. Bonita was dead and so was the past.

"Thanks."

Cade nodded. "Mind if we hang on to your rifle?"

His eyes narrowed in concern. "You think you're in danger?"

"I can't be completely certain that her husband didn't follow us out here and strand us for reasons of his own. Before you come walking back through that door again you need to sing out."

"I'll remember that," he agreed. "Whistling nearly got me shot—and panfried."

Jayne didn't smile. She watched Zed as if he were a potentially dangerous predator.

"My foreman, Hap, is rounding up the herd west of here," Cade told him. "Talk with him privately."

"Will he believe me?"

Cade looked around for something to write on. Then he spotted his blue bandanna where he'd hung it to dry after rinsing it clean. "Give him this. He'll recognize it. Tell him not to trust anyone."

Zed frowned. Cade realized he should give Zed more of an explanation. "Before you sign on with me, you'd better know that we've had some trouble recently."

Zed's gaze flicked to Jayne who was sitting now on the bottom bunk bed watching them.

"Besides her husband," Cade clarified.

"What sort of trouble?"

"Slit girths, cut fences, fire, stampede." Cade shrugged.

"Sounds like I'm in for a nice cushy job. Let me get Lafferty saddled and I'll be right back."

When he shut the door, Jayne spoke. "I don't trust him."

"He'll be crushed. Most women trust him as soon as they meet him."

"I'm not most women."

"Truer words were never spoken."

"I'm serious." Her hand went to her injured shoulder and pressed against the bandage there, but she didn't complain even though he knew she had to be hurting.

"He's too glib. He's one of those men who uses his charm and looks to get what he wants. Obviously you two have a history. Why'd you agree to take him on?"

She wasn't taken in by his looks and charm? Cade was secretly pleased.

"Zed and I used to work the rodeo circuit together."

"I got that much."

"We were friends."

"And now you aren't. So?"

"So thanks to someone deliberately spooking the

herd the other day, I'm down two hands. Zed needs work and I have a job opening. Don't worry, I'll watch him.''

''I wasn't worried. It's not my problem. I'd just be careful, that's all.''

But she obviously was worried and she looked awful.

''How do you feel?''

''Like something cats bury.''

Cade found his mood lightening. ''You do have a way with words.''

''Yeah, and I can shoot, too.''

''I'll settle for you sitting here playing with your daughter while I go outside and have a few words with our would-be rescuer,'' he explained.

''It's your neck. Just remember that our lives are currently linked to yours. Be careful. He could have another gun out back.''

''Zed isn't going to shoot me.''

''Uh-huh. I'll be sure and tell that to your next of kin.''

''I don't have any. Now, wait here.''

''Darn, and I'd planned to go shopping today.''

Cade found his lips lifting right along with his spirits as he stepped outside. She was a mouthy little thing like her daughter. But he was starting to like both of them.

That thought sobered him completely. Zed stepped around the side of the cabin leading Lafferty. The big roan snuffled a greeting and Cade rubbed his nose affectionately. ''How you doing, Laff?''

The horse whuffed and butted Cade's hand.

''Sorry, buddy. No treats today.''

''You want to tell me what the story is here, Cade?''

''No. Are you sure he's sound?''

Zed scowled, but nodded. ''He's sound. I've been

pushing hard for a couple of days and wanted to rest him. I'll do it tomorrow instead.''

"After you talk with Hap, get directions to the ranch house. Take a day and relax before you start work. For now, head due west." He indicated the direction with a flick of his wrist. "We're moving the herd east, but tell Hap I want them over this way instead."

"Should I tell him your truck was stolen?"

"May as well."

"Did you see who did it?"

"No. So tell Hap to be careful. He should spread the word that no one should leave keys in their vehicles. And have him try to catch Rio and Sven. They were heading into Darwin Crossing today. Rio has a doctor's appointment. Have Hap tell him I need disposable diapers and baby formula for a newborn. And I don't want anyone to see Rio buying the stuff. No one at all."

Zed tipped back his hat, watching Cade in some surprise. "Sure. Mind tellin' me what the deal is with you and that kid in there?"

"Yes." He didn't want to waste time with explanations.

Zed's lips tightened. Without another word he swung into the saddle and headed west. Cade watched the horse and rider out of sight. He hoped he wasn't making a costly mistake.

Zed said he'd camped nearby. Cade itched to check out the truth of that story. He turned around and found Jayne watching him from the open doorway, the baby tucked in the crook of her arm.

A shaft of pure desire caught him off guard, completely unprepared. Disheveled, wounded, married, she had an innocent sensuality that was disturbing. He wanted her. And she was just a kid!

"I told you to wait inside," he snarled.

She tipped her head to one side and her white-blond hair rippled across her shoulder like a waterfall of silk.

"No, you didn't."

"Well you should know to stay inside."

"What did he say to turn you into such a basket of cheer?"

Cade could hardly tell her it wasn't Zed, but her own effect on him that made him feel surly and annoyed. He hated being attracted to a girl young enough to be his daughter. Well, almost young enough, he amended.

"How old are you?"

"How old do you think I am?"

"Obviously too young to know better than to stand in the open doorway where you make a perfect target."

He stalked toward her. Jayne didn't back an inch.

"Hap's going to fire him," she said calmly.

Cade faltered. "What are you talking about?"

"Two minutes of conversation with Zed and you turn into a raging beast. Your friend will either have to fire Zed or shoot you." She melted back into the shack.

Cade sputtered on a laugh. It felt strange. When was the last time he'd laughed over anything? Jayne was unlike anyone he'd ever met in his life. The woman had more guts than most men he knew. And he'd known some pretty tough men in his days on the circuit.

Jayne was putting the baby down on the lower bunk when he walked inside. She looked as good from the back as she did from the front. The woman had a natural feminine grace that held none of the usual artifices. He pulled his gaze from her curvy rear end, but not before she caught him staring. He could feel the stain of heat moving up his neck.

"How old *do* you think I am?"

"You look about fourteen, going on twenty-four."

"Good guess."

Cade swore. "You *are* fourteen?" He was lusting after a fourteen-year-old?

"Of course not. I'm twenty-four."

"The hell you are."

"Fine. Have it your way. But they have a term for men who lust after fourteen-year-olds."

Cade swore again.

"Nope. That isn't it, but you're on the right track."

"I ought to turn you over my knee and paddle you."

"Yes, I saw you noting my butt. I should have figured you were the kinky sort. The quiet ones always are."

Speechless, he stared at her.

And she swayed.

"Hey!"

"I'm okay." She held up a hand to stop him. "It's just so hot in here. That's why I went to the door. I wish we could turn the fire down."

Cade looked at the banked fire and back at her. "The medicine hasn't kicked in yet. You've got a fever."

"I know."

"You should be lying down."

"You may be right."

"I was going to go down the road a piece and have a look around now that you have the rifle to defend yourself."

"I wish you wouldn't," she said before he could tell her that he'd changed his mind.

She sank gracefully onto the cot beside the baby. She shivered.

"Right now I'm not sure I could defend myself from

a marauding cockroach. I hate to go all wimpy like a woman, but…''

In three strides he was beside her. ''You're burning up again.''

''Uh-huh.''

He lifted the sleeping baby and set her in the car seat. ''Lie down.''

''Already ahead of you.''

She lay on her back, her long, silky lashes dark against her pale cheeks. They sported two bright spots of color. He'd planned to leave. To put distance between the two of them, but also to investigate their surroundings like he'd told her. Whoever stole his truck had gotten here somehow. The thief must have left some evidence behind. If Cade could just go and have a look around… But he wouldn't be going anywhere right away. Jayne couldn't take care of herself, much less the baby.

''Here, swallow this.''

Her eyes fluttered open. ''What is it?''

''The last of the aspirin unless Zed left us some.''

''I'll throw up.''

''No, you won't. Drink this.''

She didn't throw up, but it was close.

''You haven't eaten anything, that's the problem.''

''Don't mention food,'' she warned. She drank the tepid water, ignoring some that dribbled down her chin. Cade wiped it away with his fingers. She tensed and her eyes flickered open. Curious. Unafraid.

Her skin was nearly as soft as her daughter's. Jayne's eyes were a brighter blue, but they held that same trusting innocence. She lay back, closing them.

''Cade?''

''I'm right here.''

''I really am twenty-four.''

Chapter Five

Temperatures inside the cabin climbed wickedly. By midday Jayne was much too hot and she knew it wasn't due to her fever. Cade opened the front door to circulate what little air there was. The temperature was more like late June than late April.

Thanks in part to the pain pills Zed had given her, Jayne slept fitfully most of the day, waking only to eat or to watch Cade with the baby. He tended to the baby's cord and her diapers. He fed her. He played with her. And once, when he must have thought Jayne was asleep, he even sang to her in a deep pleasing baritone that made Jayne smile.

And that was the only thing to make her smile. As the day wore on her shoulder felt like someone was jamming a hot poker through it. Complaining wouldn't help a thing. She would be stoic and whimper in silence, because she'd be darned if she'd whimper in front of Cade McGovern.

Her brothers were always telling her she was too bold. Heaven knew she could never keep a boyfriend for long. Of course, she'd never found one she wanted to keep. Men were so immature.

Except maybe Cade.

He was certainly different from anyone else she knew. He was quiet like her oldest brother the judge, sure of himself like her second oldest brother the cop, and gentle like her youngest brother the trainer.

Cade fascinated her. There was a solid presence about him that was infinitely reassuring, while at the same time, totally disturbing. She decided it came more from his attitude than his hard, rugged body. Despite his gruff mannerism, he tended to the baby and her with gentle care. Why wasn't he married to some lucky woman raising a brood of his own?

Maybe he was. The thought was discouraging. Lots of men didn't wear wedding rings, especially men who did physical work outside. Neither she nor Cade had exchanged anything in the way of personal information. He wore an invisible Do Not Disturb sign plainly.

But while he tried to keep his touch impersonal, he created a whole raft of sensations inside her. And he wasn't immune. She saw the dilation of his eyes and the way he quickly drew away from any contact or sign of intimacy. She had enough experience to know he was interested, but he obviously didn't want to be.

Cade appeared to be an intensely private person. She didn't have the nerve to ask him any personal questions. That only made him more fascinating. Jayne watched silently as he paced the small cabin, only leaving the building to empty the pail in the corner.

Cade made her curious about a lot of things.

What sort of lover would he be?

Jayne chided herself for the strangely tantalizing thought, but it wouldn't go away. Fortunately, she didn't have to worry about her impulsive desire to find out. Her shoulder and the baby made a wonderful deterrent to her curiosity.

Like most newborns, Heather slept a lot. Jayne couldn't get over how tiny and precious she was. How could her mother have given her up? Likely the mother was a teenager who thought she was doing the best for her child. Jayne doubted the girl had even seen the baby before it was taken from her. She couldn't imagine holding this precious infant and then letting her go.

But as the day wore on, the baby became agitated, breaking Jayne's restless sleep. Her shoulder hurt enough that she would have liked to join in the baby's tears more than once. Only Cade's presence kept her from moaning out loud. She wouldn't let herself take a second pain pill because the first one had made her so groggy and lethargic.

By late afternoon Heather's constant crying couldn't be ignored. Cade walked the floor holding her, talking softly to no avail.

"There must be something we can do," Jayne said fretfully.

"I'm open to suggestion."

"Why don't you let me take her for a while?"

Cade eyed her. "And risk opening that shoulder again? She's just warm."

"We all are. Let me have her, Cade. My fever's down."

"For now," he agreed.

His mood was black. She suspected the pacing had more to do with his restlessness than the baby's unhappiness. He was feeling trapped here inside with them.

"You need a break. Go outside and have a look around. Take a walk. You can leave me the rifle. I assure you, I know how to use it."

"Trying to get rid of me?"

"Given your present mood, that's not a bad idea, but

I was trying to give you a break,'' she said honestly. "It's hot and miserable in this cabin. Go."

Cade hesitated. "All right, but keep the rifle at your side."

Their fingers came in contact, tangling for an instant as Cade handed her the baby. Their gazes collided. Desire burned in the depths of his eyes, reflected, she was certain, in her own heated look.

Cade jumped back as though spooked. He grabbed his hat from the table, jammed it low on his head, and strode through the door.

"Hey! Don't close that!"

"It's too dangerous otherwise. Once I'm out of sight anyone could sneak around the side of the cabin. You'd never see them until it was too late."

"We'll suffocate!"

"I won't be gone that long."

She would have argued further, but her energy for the battle faded much more quickly than her desire. It was obvious he wouldn't leave unless he could close the front door and he needed a break, if only from the baby's incessant cries. The man could give stubborn lessons to her brothers.

"Can we at least open the window?"

"I tried. It's nailed shut. Sorry. I won't be long. I just want a quick look around. If anyone opens that door without calling out, shoot 'em."

"Yeah, right."

"I'm serious, Jayne. We don't know what's going on here. I'm not leaving if you can't follow orders."

"Don't worry, I won't do anything that will jeopardize the baby." That much, at least, was true.

She stared at the closed door long after he disappeared. She'd been right. Cade definitely felt the same attraction she felt. But that big moody man and her? Not likely. He still wasn't even convinced she was an adult.

And if he became convinced?

The appealing thought was disturbing. She wasn't vain, but most men were interested in her looks. Few ever looked any deeper. Somehow, she thought Cade would.

The idea of kissing those hard firm lips was tremendously exciting and scary at the same time. She'd never dated anyone remotely like Cade. Her father and brothers had always seen to it that she left the cowboys strictly alone. That had never bothered her since she'd never seen one as interesting as Cade.

The banker, Realtor, and CPA she'd been dating recently didn't compare with Cade. She doubted very many men did. Jayne was pretty sure her family never would have let her within a mile of someone like this cowboy.

She disciplined her thoughts and rocked the crying baby in her good arm. Her shoulder hurt. The thought had become nearly a litany and the sound of the baby's crying was grating on her nerves.

What if there was something seriously wrong with the baby? What if she was getting sick? Jayne couldn't stand the thought of her in this sort of distress.

"Look, little one, don't you dare be getting sick, okay? We aren't any happier with this situation than you are, but screaming won't do a thing except make you ill. Believe me, if I thought it would help, I'd join you. What do you say we get this diaper off and let you lie there naked for a while, huh? I wouldn't mind being naked in this heat, either."

But she suspected Cade would object. If she'd embarrassed him by mentioning that she'd caught him staring at her butt, she could imagine how he'd look if he walked in and found her naked.

Being naked with Cade McGovern.

Now there was a thought to send thrills up a woman. Chills! She'd meant chills!

Or had she?

It was the fever. She was having crazy thoughts because she was so weak and sick.

"What do you think of him, little girl? I saw you flirting with him earlier, flashing that innocent little baby smile at him. You've got good taste, but he's too old for you. He thinks he's too old for me, too."

But he wasn't. He couldn't be more than mid to late thirties. And Cade was the stuff of adolescent fantasies come to life. Tall, broad shouldered, rugged, he was simply gorgeous. That thick, rich, dark hair tempted innocent fingers to have their way. And that aura of self-confidence was a powerful draw in itself. Which meant he must have tons of women coming on to him. One more reason why she needed to fight this attraction.

She set the baby on the bed and got the diaper off without jarring her shoulder too much, but the crying didn't stop.

"Oh, sweetie, please don't cry like this. You're really scaring me. How about this? What if I sponge you off to cool you down and give you some sugar water? I know you aren't hungry, but I sort of remember Mom saying something about giving babies sugar water. I don't think it can hurt anything."

Jayne pushed aside her growing concern and reached for the bottled water. Her blouse was already ruined, so she moistened the hem and began sponging off the baby. Instantly, the infant seemed to calm.

Undoing several of the buttons on her borrowed shirt she patted down her own chest with the water. Her bra got wet, but she ignored it because the water did help.

"I should have thought of this sooner, baby." Taking a deep breath, she struggled out of her slacks. "Ah, even better."

Barefoot, with Cade's shirt hanging mostly open, she began the sugar hunt. Fortunately, she found the tightly sealed tin without too much trouble. The effort required to get it open was a little frightening. She felt so dizzy afterward it scared her. She was never ill.

The baby's whimpers faded completely as she alternated dampening the infant and then herself. The cooling cloth made them both feel better and the sugar water seemed to go over well, too.

Jayne lay down beside the infant, biting her lip when she moved wrong and sent fire down her arm. She hoped Zed would bring rescue soon. She cradled the infant and yawned. It had been a while since she'd taken the pain pill and all she'd done was sleep all day, yet it was still hard to keep her eyes open.

"Jayne? I'm coming in."

Cade entered slowly and stopped. He surveyed the bed with an expression she couldn't read. His eyes were hidden beneath the brim of his hat. No question about it. Cade was dangerously attractive. Her heart gave a peculiar flutter just looking at him. With his hat pulled low like that, dressed in those snug-fitting jeans and boots, a toothpick jutting from the corner of his mouth, he could have posed for one of those sexy billboard ads. His entire stance shouted seductive cowboy stud, and she'd take bets he didn't even realize that fact.

His expression was peculiar. It took her muzzy brain a few seconds to remember that her legs were bare and the shirt was undone far enough to be provocative. Not only that, the shirt had several damp spots from the wet bra clinging to the fabric.

Oh, no. Did he think she was trying to appear seductive? With this shoulder?

"Guess it takes a mother's touch," he said mildly as she sat up gingerly, pulling the shirt closed.

"I gave us a sponge bath," she explained.

Cade grunted, but his gaze remained fixed as if he couldn't bear to look away. Her nipples responded to that expression while her stomach tightened in crazy anticipation.

"I also made her some sugar water," she added hastily.

Cade frowned, momentarily diverted. "Is that good for her?"

"I don't see how it can hurt."

"Do you want me to finish changing her while you get dressed?"

Well, that was pointed enough. She almost asked him why she'd want to get dressed, but she was a little leery of provoking him too far. As she reached for her slacks she realized how much of her body was actually exposed. Not only were her legs bare, but his shirt gaped dangerously. No wonder he was staring.

"I was trying to let the air get to her bottom before we have to deal with diaper rash," she said trying to ignore the heat rising in her cheeks as her fingers fumbled with buttons.

His jaw clenched. "Do you need help putting your pants back on?"

Surprised by his tone, she lifted her head. His look of irritation raised her hackles. She set the pants beside her and finished buttoning the too big shirt to a more respectable level. To heck with worrying about provoking him.

"Why would I need help? I plan to leave them off. It's too hot in here."

Cade muttered something under his breath. She had a feeling it wasn't complimentary.

"Hap's on his way with the truck. I saw him from the hill out back. He should be here in a few minutes. While I'm sure he'd appreciate your lack of attire, you need to get dressed. We're leaving."

"Then how come you look so mad? I thought you'd be happy to get rid of us."

Cade scowled. "Get dressed, Jayne."

As he moved around the cabin collecting things, Jayne struggled to get her stained, dirty slacks back on. She had to take several deep breaths to keep from crying out when her shoulder protested, but she finally managed. For the first time she became conscious of how disheveled and mussed she looked. Her hair was matted with blood and she was dirty and sticky and she smelled sweaty. She must be getting better if she could worry about her looks.

"Can I help?" she asked him.

He turned around. "You're doing it. Just keep Heather happy and I'll set this stuff on the porch. Then I'll come in and get her ready to go."

"Okay."

Now that rescue was at hand, Jayne couldn't decide what she was feeling. Relief, certainly, but it was sort of bittersweet. This Hap person would drive her into town and she'd probably never see Cade again. Only, she didn't want Cade to disappear from her life. Cade attracted her as no other man ever had.

But she couldn't deny that he seemed more than

ready to get rid of her and the baby. Who could blame him? She'd been nothing but trouble from the start. And it dawned on her that maybe that trouble wasn't quite over yet.

"Cade, about the man who shot me—"

He jammed the empty baby bottle that he'd washed back inside the diaper bag without looking at her. "Save it for the sheriff."

His words made her blink in surprise. He'd grown more moody and more remote than ever since he'd come back inside the cabin. What had turned him so surly?

"But you should know—"

"No. I shouldn't know." He shot her a glare from beneath the brim of his hat. "As soon as Hap gets here, I'm going to have him radio the sheriff. You can give the sheriff all the details of your problems. My job is done once you're safely in his hands."

She felt as if he'd slapped her. His words seemed to come out of the blue. His tone was implacable. He acted as if he didn't care about her any longer. All the warm cozy thoughts Jayne had been harboring about the sexy cowboy died a swift death. She bent her head over the baby to hide the sting of tears. She heard him curse.

"Look, I'm sorry if I hurt your feelings," he growled.

"Forget it," she managed to respond, glad that her voice came out strong. "You made your point."

Cade swore under his breath.

"You ought to try to broaden your vocabulary," she told him, standing up and willing the dizziness not to betray her weakness in front of him. "Heather and I are going to wait outside on the porch. The air in here is too thick to breathe."

He stiffened instantly. "You'll stay in here until Hap gets here."

"Make me."

For a moment they glared at one another like a pair of little kids. While she felt foolish—a smart person doesn't tease a mountain lion—she was determined not to back down no matter what he said.

"Fine," Cade agreed abruptly. "Go ahead and make a target of yourself, but leave your daughter in here so I can get her ready to go."

"Fine."

But it wasn't fine. She didn't want this stupid cowboy to dislike her. She looked at Heather. The baby was staring around in innocent contentment. She was so precious and beautiful. Jayne realized she was going to miss the little girl. Jayne kissed her forehead and winced as she moved wrong and the shoulder sent pain streaming down her arm again.

"You all right?"

She waited for the spasm to pass, then she lifted the rifle. "I'll wait for you outside." And she strode past Cade without looking at him. She was very much afraid if she did, she'd burst into tears—and not from the pain.

Outside, dusk was descending. The weather was much too hot, but the land was beautiful with the hills still flush with bluebonnets. She'd always loved the peaceful serenity of her parents' ranch, but Cade's land was breathtaking. Too bad he had turned out to be an insensitive jerk. She was certain now that he wasn't married. Who would put up with his inexplicable mood swings? Not even to live on land like this. Uh-uh. No way.

His cows probably didn't like him, either.

By the time the man he introduced as Hap Ramirez

pulled up outside the cabin, she was more than ready to see a friendly face. Only his wasn't. Hap was a stocky, barrel-chested man of about sixty with weathered skin, dark piercing eyes and a dour expression that assessed her and the baby without a blink.

"Lithcolm told the truth, after all," Hap said as he greeted Cade.

"You came alone?" Jake demanded.

"I thought it best from what I was told. And there wasn't time to unload the truck so there was no room for anyone else. It'll be dark soon and I want to get back to the men and the herd as quickly as possible."

Jake nodded. "We need to get Jayne and her baby to Doc Zimmerman."

Hap's perpetual scowl deepened. "This is his week to go visit his daughter, did you forget?"

Jake swore. "Yeah. I did. Okay. We'll radio the—"

But Hap was shaking his head.

"What?" Jake demanded. "Don't tell me your radio isn't working."

"Not anymore. The wires were cut shortly after I spoke to Zed. They can be repaired but it will take time."

Jake strode to the vehicle using a string of epitaphs that were more impressive than the ones her brother the cop had used the day he fell off the roof.

"The wires were cut after Zed arrived?"

Hap's eyes narrowed. "Yeah."

"Who else was around?"

"I saw no one but our own people."

Cade's jaw set in a hard line. Jayne shivered at his expression. He thought Zed was responsible. But if that was true then why had the cowboy sent help?

"Where's Zed now?" he asked in a quiet, deadly voice.

"He said you instructed him to go to the ranch."

Jayne saw Cade's fingers close in a fist. "I did," he stated bleakly. "Okay. I'll deal with Zed later. We'll have to take Jayne into the city."

Without moving a muscle, Hap managed to express his shock. "That's a very long drive."

Cade eyed him steadily. "Then we'd better get going."

He couldn't have made his desire to get rid of her quickly any plainer. Before she could tell him not to do her any favors, Hap shook his head.

"As you wish, however, they're predicting severe thunderstorms between here and there with heavy rain, lightning, flash floods. There's even a tornado watch in effect."

"Now when was the last time we had a tornado in this part of Texas?"

Hap shrugged. All three of them looked toward the sky and the swiftly moving clouds building over the hills.

"We can undoubtedly make the city, but returning home again..." Hap shrugged once more.

Cade uttered another oath. "All right," he said grudgingly. "We'll go to the house. I can take them first thing in the morning. I guess one more day won't matter."

Jayne stood straighter in an effort not to show any weakness. "Don't worry about me. I'll be fine."

As soon as she could get to a phone she could call one of her brothers to come get her. Belatedly it occurred to her that if anyone had spotted her car sitting in the parking lot of that shopping center with her belongings scattered all over, her family must be worried sick by now. Funny, this was the first time she'd even considered that aspect of her situation.

"I was concerned about your daughter," Cade said mildly.

Chastised, Jayne blinked back tears. She never cried. Never. Turning away, she felt totally enervated.

"You did get hold of Rio, right?" Cade asked Hap.

Hap grunted an assent. "He wasn't pleased, but he should be on his way back with the items you requested."

"I don't pay him to be pleased," Cade snapped. "I pay him to follow orders. I may need a couple of the men to stand guard when we get back to the house in case Rio wasn't as discreet as he was told to be. The lady has a husband out gunning for her. Literally. He's already put one hole in her. I don't aim to give him another crack."

"I can take care of myself," she said stoutly. Neither man so much as looked her way.

"We're already down two men," Hap reminded Cade sourly. "If the weather changes course and comes in this direction I'll need every man I've got and then some to keep those ornery cows together."

"Let me have Rio and Sven since neither of them can ride herd right now anyhow."

"Sven left," Hap said acerbically. "He said your ranch is jinxed."

Cade set his jaw. "Let's load up and get out of here."

Despite his surly disposition, Jayne was sorry to be causing Cade extra problems. It sounded like he had enough of his own. For the life of her, Jayne couldn't figure out why Zed would cut the radio lines in Hap's truck.

Unless he was part of the kidnapping ring.

The thought paralyzed her, but it made a crazy kind of sense. Lily Garrett had told her the ring was part of a large criminal organization. That meant anyone could be involved.

Even Zed.

But then why hadn't he taken the baby from them when he first arrived? Was he afraid of Cade? The two men were of a similar size and build, but Cade moved with a quiet force she suspected would give him an edge in any physical battle. Of course, Zed looked as if he could take care of himself as well. The bottom line was that she wouldn't want to see the two men go at one another. She had a feeling the results would be much uglier than the day two of her brothers got into a fight over a girl they both wanted to date.

She put a hand to her aching head. Her thoughts were muddled. She wanted to tell Cade what she suspected about Zed, but he didn't want to know about her problems. All he wanted was to get her off his land. That would probably be best for all of them.

Jayne pushed the hurt aside and eyed the battered green pickup truck. The vehicle didn't look like it would make it to the main road, let alone any distance beyond that point. Fortunately, Jayne knew how deceiving looks could be when it came to ranch trucks. Her dad had one she'd swear was used before World War I.

The baby carrier wouldn't fit in the back so Cade rigged it for the passenger seat. That meant she had to scrunch in the back with Cade. Jayne thought about protesting, but both men were already grim. Besides, the air-conditioning was a blessed relief and made the tight quarters bearable.

Jayne sat back with a sigh, all too aware of the friction of Cade's hard, muscled thigh pressed tightly against her own as the truck bounced over the rough terrain. He held himself stiffly, so she pulled as far away as she could manage. Half the back seat had been taken up by a pile of objects including an old saddle. They couldn't put it in the bed because the back of the truck was already piled high with baling wire and fence posts and other items. She was grateful Cade hadn't suggested she ride on the roof.

"You doing okay?" he asked abruptly.

Each jolt of the truck sent hot embers of pain down her arm. Cade must have noticed her grimace, or maybe it was the way she had curled her fists until her nails bit into the skin of her palms. But she'd pass out before she complained.

"Don't worry. I'll be out of your hair just as soon as I can reach a telephone."

His steady gaze pinned her. "Got someplace to go?"

"Yes."

He waited, but she closed her eyes to signify the end of the conversation. A petty victory to be sure, but she savored it. After a moment, he directed the next question to Hap.

"Anything else I should know about?"

"We found three more sections of fence down—all on different sides. We've got critters scattered from one end of this spread to the other."

Cade growled.

His problems were none of her business, Jayne told herself, but she knew that her presence was keeping him from his own work.

"How'd he get to the radio without being noticed?" Cade muttered.

"We'll have to catch him to ask."

"I intend to."

And the quiet emphasis in Cade's tone sent a shiver down her spine. He definitely thought Zed was responsible.

"You ready to call the sheriff yet?" Hap demanded. "Or are you going to wait until someone gets seriously hurt? Maybe a poisoned well or another stampede. We're going to start losing cattle and men if we don't catch him soon, Cade. Some of the new hires are starting to talk like Sven. If the Circle M gets a reputation, you won't be able to hire anyone."

"I'll call the sheriff as soon as we reach the house," Cade promised harshly.

Hap didn't respond. The baby began to whimper.

"I hope to hell Rio got some baby formula in town," Cade muttered.

THE ONE-STORY ranch house wasn't pretty. The faded white clapboard needed a coat of paint, a carpenter, a landscaper or perhaps simply a demolition crew, she thought uncharitably. She eyed the old washing machine sitting on the front porch.

The building did have indoor plumbing and real beds with sheets that looked clean. That automatically ranked it above the line shack, Jayne decided. As she peered around, she concluded that no woman had ever lived in the house. At least not for any extended period of time. The furniture was utilitarian and undusted, though surprisingly uncluttered. And there were none of the little touches necessary to turn the place into something resembling a home. Cade was definitely not married.

This was a house where men hung their clothing and periodically rested their boots on the old scarred furniture while they drank a beer and watched television. The rooms were neater than she would have expected. And the bathroom and kitchen were actually clean enough that she didn't have to worry about touching surfaces.

She cradled the sleeping baby in her good arm and wished she could close her eyes as well. It was a major effort to stand up. The trip to the ranch house had exhausted her reserves and all she wanted to do was sleep.

Her secret fear that Zed would be lying in ambush when they arrived proved false. If he was working for the kidnappers, he was in no hurry to claim the baby. She didn't even see Zed.

The idea of another pain pill was looking better by the moment. Cade and Hap were arguing as they came inside with the last load from the truck.

"When did that happen?" Cade was asking Hap.

Jayne wondered what else had gone wrong.

"Could have been any time. We don't have the manpower to watch every inch of this spread. You know that, Cade."

"Then we'll hire more crew."

"From where? You going to manufacture some out of thin air?"

Cade and Hap glared at one another.

"Excuse me, but could one of you tell me where to find a telephone before you come to blows?" And before she curled herself in a ball and cried herself to sleep.

"In the kitchen," Cade snapped. "On the wall by the desk."

"Thank you. You're too kind."

Hap rolled his eyes and turned and stalked back out the front door.

"I'll get the sheriff's number for you," Cade added gruffly.

She knew his anger wasn't directed at her, but it annoyed her all the same. "That won't be necessary."

He laid a broad hand on her good shoulder to stop her just short of the kitchen. The action jarred the baby and her injured shoulder. Fortunately, Heather didn't wake.

"Sorry. But it is necessary, Jayne. You're going to report this incident to the sheriff. The guy shot you. I don't care if he is Heather's father, you can't just pretend it didn't happen."

Jayne straightened her posture. She looked pointedly at his work-roughened hand where it rested against the shirt. Slowly, Cade released her. Something sparked in his eyes, but was quickly hidden from view. She was in no mood to spar with the surly cowboy, but she wasn't about to let him bulldoze her, either.

"I don't intend to pretend it didn't happen," she said quietly. "Believe me, I'll see he gets what he deserves, but you said you didn't want to know any details so I won't bore you with any. I can handle it from here."

She spotted the telephone, then realized she couldn't dial the phone and hold the baby at the same time. Cade came to the same conclusion.

"I'll take her."

"Thank you."

This time there was no physical reaction to his touch. She wouldn't allow it. Cade wanted her gone and she wanted that, too. She pushed the familiar buttons, aware that he watched her.

When she brought the phone to her ear there was no sound. She waited a second and still nothing, so she hung up.

"No one home?"

"The call didn't go through."

She picked up the receiver again and put it to her ear. "There's no dial tone."

"Let me have that!"

Cade took it in his empty hand and held the receiver to his own ear.

"Don't you dare swear while you're holding the baby," she warned before he could utter the curse she saw forming on his lips.

"Take her."

For all his irritation, he handed her the baby with tempered care. Then he strode down the hall bellowing Hap's name. Jayne followed in his wake. There was no sign of Hap as she stepped onto the front porch. Cade didn't pause. He crossed the porch, put one hand on the railing and swung himself over the rail, landing lightly on the ground at the side of the house. Jayne followed curiously. She leaned over to see what he was doing.

Cade paused next to the air-conditioning unit and bent down to look at something. When he stood, there was murder in his eyes.

"Cade?"

"Someone cut the phone line."

The hairs on the back of her neck and along her arms raised in alarm. *Was* Zed part of the baby ring?

It was possible. The man in the silver car must have noted Cade's license plate back at the feed store. That would have led him right here. She'd just put Cade and Hap and everyone associated with this ranch in grave danger.

Maybe Cade didn't want to know the details of her shooting, but he was going to listen to her nonetheless. But before she could say anything, a cloud of dust caught her attention. A white SUV roared up the rutted road leading to the house.

"Cade?"

"Get inside! No, wait. It's okay. It's Rio."

Her heart pounded against the back of her throat. "Are you sure?"

"Yeah. That's Rio."

"Cade?" Hap called running up.

"Someone cut the phone lines," Cade told him.

"Barn, too. I was coming to tell you that."

"Where's Zed?" Cade demanded.

"I would guess the bunkhouse. His horse is in a stall."

"I'll be right back."

Hap grabbed his arm. "You need to stay with her. I'll bring him here to the house."

The SUV lurched to a stop. Hap pivoted and set off for the back of the house at a trot. A reedy young cowboy stepped down holding several grocery bags.

"Cade?" His pockmarked features stared at Cade in shock. "How did you beat me back here?"

"What are you talking about?"

"I coulda swore I saw your truck outside Sully's when I went past."

Cade moved toward him so fast the man called Rio flinched back as if expecting to get hit.

"You saw my truck outside Sully's? Today?"

"Well, yeah. As I was leavin' town. I mean, I thought it was yours. Had that same dent in the right front fender. It was sittin' right there in plain sight."

"Did you see who was driving it?"

"No one was driving it, Cade. It was just parked there, you know? Kind of off in the corner by the trees. I just wondered why—"

"And you didn't see anyone near it?"

He pushed back his hat and scratched his head. "No. There wasn't nobody around at all."

Cade's gaze flew to her. "I think we can safely rule out your husband as a car thief."

Rio gaped, plainly at a loss.

"How do you figure that?" she demanded, not bothering to try to correct his assumption.

"We didn't pass his car on our way back to the ranch. I was watching for it. He would have had to drive close to the line shack in order to steal the truck. Must have been a drifter after all."

"Someone stole your truck?" Rio asked sounding dumbfounded.

"And left us stranded out at the line shack."

"Oh, wow. I wonder if it was that kid Terry said was askin' about you over at Sully's."

Chapter Six

"What kid?" Cade demanded, but a cold certainty settled in the pit of his stomach.

Luís.

"Hey, take it easy, man. I don't know what kid. Terry said some Mexican kid was askin' for directions to the Circle M. A young kid."

"How young?"

"Beats me. Terry just said young. He figured the kid was a runaway lookin' for work."

Or an ex-brother-in-law looking to cause trouble?

"When was this?" he asked Rio.

Rio shoved his hat up on his head and scratched at the exposed thatch of hair. "Terry didn't say."

"I don't suppose he gave you any kind of description of the kid."

"No. If I'd known it was important, I woulda asked."

There was no point in taking out his frustration on Rio any more than on Jayne like he'd been doing since he walked into the line shack and saw her looking like something out of a men's magazine. Guilt gnawed on him. He'd acted like a jerk because he wanted her. He was pretty sure she hadn't set the scene to provoke him, only he couldn't forget the way Bonita had liked to manipulate him. Who knew what a woman was thinking?

Glancing at Jayne now, he realized she looked done in completely. He had a feeling only her pride was holding her upright.

"Never mind."

"You think this kid stole your truck?" Rio asked.

"He would have needed a horse or a four-wheel drive to get out to where we were. We didn't see any signs of another vehicle so if it was him, he must have tethered a horse near the road and walked in."

"And did what with the horse?" Jayne suddenly asked. "I don't think a horse could climb into the back of your truck."

"No, but he could have been tied to the bumper and led back to town."

"Why?" Rio asked pushing back his hat to scratch his head. "This got somethin' to do with all the stuff goin' on around here?"

"Maybe."

"You know who the kid is," Jayne stated.

She saw entirely too much despite her injury. He was starting to think she hadn't lied about being twenty-four.

"I know who I think he might be," Cade corrected her. "I need to get into town to find out if I'm right."

The desire to jump in the SUV and head back to Darwin Crossing was powerful, but he had to take care of Jayne first and find out what his good buddy Zed knew about things like cut telephone lines.

"Your friend Terry didn't say where the kid was staying, did he?" Cade asked.

"No, but there aren't too many places to stay around here unless he's campin' out."

And that left a whole lot of territory.

Rio shifted nervously. "Uh, Cade, did you know Sven quit?"

"Hap told me."

"Well, uh, some of the others are startin' to get worried, too. I mean with all that's been happenin' and everything. You know, the fire, the stampede…"

Cade struggled not to show his thoughts. "Does that include you, Rio?" he asked quietly.

"No. No. I was just sayin'…"

Rio squirmed under Cade's steady gaze and shook his head. Cade found Jayne watching the scene beneath half-closed eyes. Her features were ghostly pale. She was fading fast.

Cade turned to her. "You need to go to bed before you fall down."

Her injury hadn't affected her ability to glare.

"Rio, see if Hap needs help. I want to talk with my old friend, Zed."

And this time when he got his hands on Zed, he was going to do more than knock the bronco rider across a room. Was it possible that Zed and Luís were working together?

Rio disappeared with a nervous darting glance at Jayne. Apparently her glare made an impression on him. She swayed slightly and Cade reached for her, but she jerked back out of range.

"I was only going to take Heather," Cade lied.

Without a word, she relinquished the infant. Their fingers brushed. As had happened before, touching her had a strange effect on his senses. He wanted to draw her closer, to hold her and keep her pain at bay.

"Come on," he said in grouchy defiance of his inner thoughts. "Bedrooms are down the hall. I need another look at that shoulder."

"No."

Her eyes burned with determination as well as fever, but she led the way down the hall, stopping when he indicated his grandfather's room. She didn't comment on the room, not that there was all that much to notice. His grandfather hadn't spent any time on homey touches. Until this moment, Cade hadn't given much thought to changing that.

This was the largest of the three bedrooms. Jayne watched silently while he pulled back the covers on the double bed and set Heather down on the far side.

"I'll help you get undressed," he offered.

"No."

Just the one word as she held his gaze.

"Suit yourself. I need to take care of a couple of things, then I'll make you something to eat."

He strode to the kitchen and filled a large glass with ice water. When he returned, he found she'd toed off her shoes and was sitting on the edge of the bed looking lost and very young. Her spine straightened and she raised her head the instant she realized he was there. Proud defiance gleamed in her feverish eyes.

"You need another pill."

She didn't respond, but she held out her hand for the antibiotic. He added a pain tablet and she swallowed them down without comment, draining the glass of water.

"Can I do anything else for you? Bring you something else to drink?"

"No."

She needed fluids, but she'd only argue with him in her current mood. "All right." He tried for a softer tone and resisted an urge to touch her again. She looked so fragile. His careless words earlier had hurt her, he realized. He wanted to explain why he'd been so abrupt but wasn't sure that he could.

"I'm sorry about earlier, Jayne."

He hadn't meant to say that. The words just tripped past his brain. He should get out of here before he said something stupid. But he was inexplicably drawn to her when he shouldn't be thinking any such thing. She simply looked at him.

"Get some rest. We'll talk later."

"Just remember that your friend didn't have to give me this medication," she said unexpectedly. "Before you beat Zed to a pulp, you might want to listen to what he has to say."

"I thought you didn't trust Zed."

"I don't. Not for a minute. He's entirely too smooth. But I do believe in innocent until proven guilty. Would you close the door on your way out?"

Her dismissal hurt almost as much as her indictment. The latter, probably because it was so close to the truth. He had planned to sink his fist in Zed's face and ask questions afterward.

If only he hadn't brushed her off when Jayne had tried to talk to him. Certainly he hadn't done it for the reason she must be thinking. The truth was, he hadn't wanted to know about her with another man. And his reasons why didn't bear examination right now.

"If you want to talk—"

"I'll save it for the sheriff."

He sighed and ran a hand across his jaw, rubbing the stubble growing there. "I'll be back," he said quietly.

Jayne didn't bother to open her eyes.

In the living room, Zed stood between Hap and Rio. His expression was tight with suppressed emotion. "Do

I get a hearing before you beat the hell outta me?'' he demanded as soon as he saw Cade.

Jayne's caution replaced the anger that churned in Cade's chest. She was right. He didn't know that Zed had anything to do with the problems at the Circle M. There were crease marks down one side of the bronco rider's face as if he'd been sleeping on his side. They were fading rapidly beneath his spreading anger.

"Bunkhouse lines were cut, too," Hap said fiercely.

"And I'm responsible, huh?" Zed responded.

"You were the only one here," Hap replied.

"Take it easy, Hap. What do you know about the phone lines being cut?" Cade asked.

"Nothing but what your foreman said, but I don't expect you'll believe that. I stabled Lafferty, went over to the bunkhouse, took a shower and fell asleep. I didn't see or hear a thing."

Hap snorted. Rio shifted, looking puzzled. His gaze went from one man to the next. Zed stood defiantly, legs spread, hands at his sides. And it was his expression that made Cade hesitate. Zed didn't expect to be believed. And he *had* taken a shower. He'd even shaved.

Because of Jayne?

Cade shoved that thought aside. "You didn't see anyone when you rode up?" he asked.

"No," Zed replied bitterly.

Cade expelled a long breath. "Okay."

"Okay?" Hap gaped at him. "What do you mean, okay?"

"The lines could have been cut at any time," Cade explained. "We don't know when it happened. I haven't made any calls in a couple of days, have you?"

"But—"

"I'll use the radio in the SUV and try to raise the sheriff's office. We'll let them investigate the situation. You'd better get back to the herd, Hap. Move them over toward the line shack. I laid in some extra supplies over there. Zed and Rio can stay here tonight and I'll send Zed out to help you in the morning when I drive Jayne and her daughter into town."

Anger flared in Hap's expression. His lips compressed in a thin white line. Zed appeared shocked by Cade's words, while Rio simply looked puzzled by it all.

"I would do things differently if I were running this ranch," Hap stated. "I hope you know what you are doing, amigo." He pivoted and strode out the front door, letting the screen bang shut behind him. Cade would have to find a way to smooth things over with the older man later. He knew in some ways, Hap resented Cade's authority. But he was a good foreman. More like part of the family than hired labor.

"Thanks," Zed said.

Their eyes locked. Cade inclined his head. "Don't make me sorry. If I find out you had anything to do with what's been happening here, Zed, I'll make the bull that hurt you look like a pussycat."

Zed's body tightened, but he gave no other outward sign of his thoughts.

"I need you and Rio to make a complete sweep of the area," Cade continued. "If someone is hiding nearby I want him found. If more trouble has been rigged, I want it discovered. Take your rifle," he told Zed. "Have you got a firearm, Rio?"

Rio blinked in surprise. "Yeah. Sure, Cade."

"Keep it on you, but don't shoot anyone unless your life is threatened, got it?"

"Sure, Cade. But...I mean...do you think we need guns?"

"I hope not, but sooner or later, someone is going to get hurt. I don't want it to be one of my people. Are the keys in the SUV?"

Rio's head bobbed.

"I'll try to reach the sheriff. Holler if you see anyone or if anything looks wrong."

"Sure. Okay."

Zed simply nodded.

Cade followed the men outside, handing Zed the rifle. He reached for the radio and stopped. Fingers of fear lifted his hair and coiled his gut.

"Rio!" he shouted, even as he squatted down for a look under the dash. Torn wires dangled uselessly.

Both men turned back in concern. Cade stood and shut the door carefully. His gaze swept the perimeter around the house. Zed did the same, his stance alert, the rifle in a half-raised position.

"When's the last time you used the radio, Rio?"

"When Hap called and told me to pick up that stuff for you. Why?"

"You didn't use it after you went into the store?"

Rio shook his head. Zed met his gaze head-on. "If someone got to that, too, I guess it lets me out."

"I guess it does. They yanked the wires out. It'll be a job to fix."

"I didn't know!" Rio immediately protested. "I didn't use it, honest, Cade."

"Did you see anyone near the SUV when you were in town?"

"No. But I wasn't watchin' it."

"You figure it happened in town or out here?" Zed asked quietly.

"I'd give a lot to know that answer," Cade said.

"Whoever it was would have had to be fast. We were standin' right inside the door. And Hap just left."

The trail of dust he'd raised was still visible. And Cade had no way to call him back and let him know. "More than likely it happened in town." *Luís.* "But let's have a look around to be sure."

Zed shook his head.

"What?"

"You gotta stay here. You can't leave the woman and the baby inside unprotected. Rio and I will search."

It went against every instinct, but Cade knew he was right. He couldn't risk Jayne or Heather. "Come back here when you're finished."

Zed nodded. "Come on, Rio."

Looking spooked, Rio fell into step beside Zed. Cade turned and went back inside. Could he trust Zed?

Did he have a choice?

Cade walked through the house checking every room, every closet, every place a person could hide and every place a person could have tampered with something. He came up empty. His last stop was the room Jayne occupied. He found her sitting on the edge of the bed, struggling with buttons, the silvery thread of tears reflected on her cheeks.

"Want some help?"

She brushed her cheeks before looking up. "I can't get the stupid thing off." Her voice was weak and her fingers were shaking.

"I'll do it."

"I hate being helpless!"

"I know the feeling."

"Something else happened, didn't it?"

Her eyes were tiny pinpoints. The pain pill had taken

effect, but it hadn't dulled her brain completely. Tersely, he told her.

"That doesn't make sense."

"I have an enemy. It doesn't have anything to do with you."

"But what's the point?"

He shook his head. "I'm not sure. I was having problems long before you made the unfortunate choice of my truck."

"I didn't have any options," she snapped.

And he knew she'd taken his words wrong. Before he could apologize her expression changed.

"You don't think it's Zed anymore, do you?"

"Not unless he's got an accomplice. He couldn't be in two places at once. Don't worry. Nothing's going to happen to you and Heather. Zed and Rio and I will take turns keeping watch tonight. In the morning we'll take the SUV into town and get you some medical attention. I'll turn the situation over to the local sheriff and let him deal with this. Now let's get that shirt off so you can get some sleep."

When he sat on the bed beside her the air seemed to infuse with sensual awareness. She watched him from under a fringe of dark eyelashes that didn't quite veil her instant reaction to his hands on her. Well, he'd known she felt the same attraction he did. It was up to him to ignore that attraction and keep everything impersonal.

"I wish I could tell you to go away," she said quietly, "but I appreciate your help. I feel as rocky and uncoordinated as a foal. I couldn't make my fingers work. You gave me another one of those pain pills didn't you?"

"You needed it."

"I must have. I didn't even notice."

He unfastened the last button and worked her arms free of the material. He tried to pretend that he didn't notice the way her bra had slipped low enough to reveal most of one sweetly curved breast and the puckered nipple that drew his gaze like a magnet.

"Sure you don't want me to take a look at the shoulder?"

"No. I'm so tired I can't keep my eyes open. It's too hot in here."

"Part of that's the fever talking, but I'll turn on the ceiling fan. Can you stand up? I'll help you slide your pants down."

No doubt about it, he was a glutton for punishment. Touching her like this was half killing him. His body all but vibrated with a longing to touch her very differently.

She stood unsteadily and so did he. He reached for the button on her pants, but her fingers were already there. The shaft of desire caught him off guard. He'd thought he was under control, but touching her bare skin was pushing that control to its limits. She wasn't trying to be the least bit provocative, just the opposite, in fact. This was his libido working overtime.

"I can do this part," she said. Her long blond hair fell over her good shoulder giving her a sexy, abandoned air that was highly erotic. Being this close to her was playing havoc with his common sense.

"I'd better do it," he said gruffly. "Pulling them down will hurt your arm. Don't worry. I won't attack you."

"I didn't think you would."

She was too trusting. She didn't know him. And she hadn't noticed what being this close to her was doing to certain parts of his anatomy or she wouldn't be so complacent, fever or no fever.

Her cheeks flamed as his fingers brushed the soft bare skin at her waist. The touch was electrifying. Their eyes met and held.

"I don't think this is a good idea," she said breathlessly.

"Yeah. Me, either."

With a deep breath, he stilled his racing pulse and quickly undid the button and the zipper. In one fast motion he slid the pants down her legs, trying not to notice their shape or her low-riding panties. She certainly didn't look like a woman who had just given birth. She looked young and sexy with a tight firm body he longed to explore. If he'd ever given it any thought he would have figured it took weeks for a woman to get her shape back. Must be the incredible resiliency of youth.

"Sit back on the bed," he ordered roughly.

She complied without a sound. He knelt to remove her pants as fast as he could. He was even noticing that she had nice feet, delicately formed like the rest of her. This was no good. No good at all. He had no business wanting her like this.

But he did.

Cade stood quickly. "I'll, uh, go find you a clean shirt you can use for a nightgown."

"I don't wear a nightgown to bed."

Hell!

There was such an air of innocence about her he couldn't believe she was deliberately baiting him.

He stood and yanked the sheet up over her, nearly falling over his own two feet in his hurry to get away from the powerful attraction he felt toward her.

"I'll wake you when dinner is ready."

Her eyes closed before her head settled against the pillow. "Thank you," she whispered.

"No problem."

Hah! Big problem. He was in lust with another man's wife. Okay, so the man should be hanged on sight, but that didn't give Cade any right to be thinking what he was thinking about Jayne. She was a kid. Off-limits!

He closed the door as he left the room and went out to the kitchen where he stood gripping the counter and trying not to picture her slim young body.

Eventually he got himself under control and put a pot of chili on to cook. He made biscuits and even threw together some brownies from a mix. And all the while he thought about Jayne. Was she really twenty-four? That still made her ten years his junior. And it didn't matter either way!

The men returned with a negative report. If someone had been lurking about, the person had gotten away clean. It was nothing less than he'd expected.

"I don't think we'll have any more problems tonight, but just to be safe, bring your gear over here tonight. There's another bed and the couch. I want us all together."

"Standin' watch might not be a bad idea," Zed suggested. "Especially if there is any chance that her husband could have tracked her here."

"I'd planned on that." But he'd forgotten all about her husband.

"Is it possible he's the one who cut your phone lines?" Zed asked.

The question seared his brain. "I assumed that was connected to the other incidents that have been happening around here, but it's possible."

"Maybe he thought Jayne was inside and wanted to keep her from calling for help."

Cade rubbed his jaw trying to think. He realized that he was nearly as tired and spent as Jayne. God knew he hadn't slept much since finding Jayne and Heather in his truck.

"Anything's possible at this point. Dinner will be ready in about thirty minutes. Go get your gear and I'll wake Jayne."

He entered the room and his heart came to a complete stop.

She'd removed her bra and kicked off the covers. His groin immediately tightened at the sight. Her features were relaxed in sleep. Unfortunately, her body beckoned with the promise of a woman.

Cade cursed under his breath. He wasn't about to wake her now. If he touched her, he was afraid he'd say or do something really stupid. Fortunately, her daughter made a terrific distraction. Heather was awake and staring around.

"Come on, little one. Let's get you in the other room before you start crying and wake your mother," he whispered. "She needs sleep more than food, though I'm sure you won't agree with that sentiment, greedy little thing that you are."

He carefully kept his eyes averted, picked up the baby and brought her out to the kitchen where he could set up her car seat. He couldn't get over this tiny human being. He was as captivated by her as he was by her mother—in an entirely different way.

Cade had never given infants or children more than a vague thought. Not even when he'd gotten married—which probably should have told him something right there. The truth was, he'd never been around children, let alone babies. Even when he lived in foster homes before his grandfather claimed him, there'd never been any little kids around.

Staring at Heather, he could see why women were so fascinated by the little tykes. Heather was incredibly sweet—perfect. No wonder her father wanted her back.

Cade changed her and got a bottle ready, but she seemed content to sit in her carrier on the kitchen table and watch.

"Cute kid," Zed said coming in the back door.

Rio stared. "She sure is awful small."

"Messy divorce?" Zed asked.

"I don't know," Cade responded truthfully. "I didn't ask." The truth was, he hadn't planned on Jayne sticking around long enough for it to matter. Now, he'd give a lot to know what he was up against where her husband was concerned. Was the man even her husband, or just a lover?

After they ate and cleaned up the kitchen Zed offered to take the first watch.

"Okay with me," Rio agreed. "I'm gonna go lie down and watch some TV in the spare room if that's okay."

Cade nodded. "Just keep the sound down so you don't wake Jayne."

"How's she doin'?" Zed asked as Cade changed Heather's diaper and picked up a baby bottle before settling down in his favorite recliner.

"Her fever was up. I gave her a couple more antibiotics and another pain pill. Are you sure you can spare them?"

"I haven't needed either in a while now, but I'm glad I still had 'em with me. She needs a doctor."

"I know."

"You look good like that," Zed said. "Kinda natural."

"Beat it, Zed."

But it did feel natural. Cade stroked the baby's soft cheek, watching as she smiled up at him, her wide blue eyes only slightly unfocused. He wondered if this was what it would be like to have a child of his own. Not that he ever would. Women and kids weren't for a loner like him. But if he did have a child, he'd want a little girl just like Heather.

And a wife like Jayne.

That thought paralyzed him. He pushed it aside, but it kept creeping back.

"She's pretty young to have a baby," Zed commented.

"Jayne claims she's twenty-four." A kid compared to his thirty-four hard years. She was soft and fragile. He was anything but.

"Still pretty young to be raisin' a kid by herself."

"Are you volunteering to take her husband's place?"

Zed raised his hands. "Not me. But I did wonder about you."

"Forget it. Once was more than enough."

The air grew silent with expectancy. Cade knew Zed was thinking about Bonita, same as he was. Jayne was different, but she'd probably be just as horrified at the idea of spending her life out here in the middle of nowhere. And why was he even thinking about this? What did it matter? Tomorrow he'd take them both into town and he'd never see either one of them again.

The thought made him restless and angry.

Zed cleared his throat. "I'm gonna go outside and have a look around."

"Good idea." Cade closed his eyes, listening to the

drone of some news show. He awoke to something warm and wet saturating his shirt and the smell of baby formula in his nose. Heather gurgled and smiled up at him.

"You threw up on me! You little monster, you," he said affectionately. "This is how you pay me back for feeding you?"

And he froze when he suddenly realized they weren't alone.

Jayne stood in the darkened hall watching him. Half her face was in deep shadows, but the part that reflected light from the kitchen was smiling. He had a feeling she'd been standing there for several minutes.

She was dressed in an old flannel shirt of his, the sleeves rolled up her arms. And from what he could see, that was the only thing she wore.

Polarized, he could only stare. The shirt hung down to midthigh. He couldn't tell if she still wore her panties or not. What he could see of her legs were bare. They were very sexy legs.

"I fell asleep," he said, oddly embarrassed at having been caught napping.

"For several hours," she agreed.

"Hours? What time is it?"

"After midnight."

No wonder he felt so stiff. "It can't be."

"Okay, then someone snuck in here and changed all your clocks."

"Not funny. Where's Zed?"

"He went outside a few seconds ago. It started raining and he wanted to have a look around."

"You must be starving." He got to his feet feeling every one of his thirty-four years.

"No. We took liberties with your kitchen. The chili was a little spicy, but good."

Zed had seen her dressed like that? "I like my chili spicy," he said gruffly.

Her eyes gleamed. "I'll remember that."

The sultry promise in her voice had nothing to do with the discussion under way. They seemed to be holding two conversations at once. Was she trying to seduce him? Was she just like Bonita?

"You won't need to remember, will you?" he asked harshly.

Her face fell. Immediately, he wished he could call the words back.

"No. I guess not. Want me to change her while you change shirts?"

"What about your shoulder?"

"My shoulder will hurt whether I change her or not. The fever's down again."

"Maybe so, but you look like you should be in bed."

She nodded seriously. "I've slept for hours, yet I feel like I could sleep for days."

"That's the body's way of healing. Want me to look at your shoulder?"

"No. It'll be okay until I can get to a doctor. Go get changed. I'll take care of her diaper. I hope you don't mind that I borrowed this from your closet. You did say—"

"That I'd get you a shirt and I forgot."

He set the baby on the couch so he wouldn't have to touch Jayne. Touching her was dangerous. It led to all sorts of crazy thoughts and ideas, like how her lips would taste, crushed beneath his own or how it would feel to have those silky legs wrapped around his body.

"You're welcome to borrow whatever you need," he

said quickly. "I'll be right back." In the bedroom he snatched up a clean shirt and pants before entering the bathroom for a quick shower. When he came out, the physical fire was doused, but mentally, he was still strongly attracted to Jayne.

Muttering an oath, he walked out into the living room only to find it still dark. No Jayne. No baby. Then he saw that her bedroom door was closed again.

He rapped lightly. "Jayne?"

"Come in."

She was sitting on the bed feeding the baby yet another bottle.

"Does she do anything besides eat and pee and throw up on unsuspecting cowboys?"

"I believe you've changed the other thing she does."

"Very funny."

Her smile tugged at his insides.

"That's what babies do. They eat, sleep and go to the bathroom. Can I ask you something, Cade?"

He inclined his head, thinking it was probably risky to let her ask anything.

"I know it's none of my business, but how come you aren't married?"

He'd been right. He should have said no.

"In case you haven't noticed, this is the middle of nowhere."

"So?"

"So women don't like living in the middle of nowhere."

"That isn't true. It's beautiful here."

"Yeah. That's what I tried to tell my wife."

Chapter Seven

So he had been married. Hadn't Jayne wondered why he wasn't? And hadn't Zed told her over dinner that he and Cade had had a falling out over a woman?

Of course, that was all Zed had said on the subject, which was a point in his favor. She wasn't really comfortable around the handsome cowboy, but his flirting seemed a matter of routine, something she could comfortably ignore, and after talking with him, she was fairly certain he had nothing to do with the black-market baby ring.

"Are you still married?" she asked Cade.

"She's dead." The lack of emotion in his voice was practically a shout.

"Oh, God. I'm sorry."

"So am I. She died in a car crash with her boyfriend after she walked out on me. He wanted to be a rodeo star. My wife was real big on rodeo stars. She didn't like ranch life."

"Oh."

That explained so many things. Zed had talked a little about their days together in the rodeo. From what he'd told her, Cade had been better than average. Well on his way toward another championship, in fact.

"That reminds me," Cade said, running a knuckle across the stubble on his chin. "I have a box of Bonita's old stuff around here somewhere. In the morning I'll dig it out. She was taller and…built differently, but there might be something in there you could use. You'd probably be more comfortable going into town in something better than one of my shirts."

Jayne wasn't sure what to say. She liked wearing his shirts, knowing he'd worn them too. Juvenile, yes, but there it was. She kept getting such mixed messages from him. His stare dared her to ask questions. And apparently he still couldn't wait to be rid of her.

"For now, you should go back to bed, Jayne. We're going to get an early start in the morning."

"You're right."

"Holler if you need anything. I'll be right next door."

Now there was a disturbing thought. "Thank you."

He let the door close quietly behind him and she settled the baby on the bed beside her. "What do you think, Heather?"

The infant gurgled up at her.

"I agree. His wife was a complete idiot."

IF IT HAD STORMED during the night, Jayne hadn't heard a thing. What she did hear was the commotion out in the hall the next morning and the less than gentle closing of the front door.

Heather lay beside her gurgling happily. Jayne had a vague memory of Cade coming in and taking the baby when she started crying, but Jayne hadn't been able to force her eyes open past her drug-aided sleep.

Any commotion around here was not a good thing. She sat up too quickly and the room canted. Her shoulder reminded her that quick actions had a penalty, but after a few moments she was able to take in the large cardboard box on the floor near the closet. Bonita's clothing.

Letting Cade see her in something his ex-wife had worn was far from her liking, but Jayne's options were severely limited. She couldn't bear to put her stained slacks back on. She rooted in the box and held up one of Bonita's bras.

No wonder Cade wasn't enamored of Jayne's charms. Jayne would need more than tissue paper to fill that cup size. Considering her shoulder, she should be grateful she was small enough and firm enough to go without a bra for now.

Cade hadn't lied about his wife's love for the rodeo. The few articles of clothing catered to that theme. All were either stained, ripped, or damaged in some way. Jayne settled on a fancy long-sleeved blouse in pale blue, trimmed in beaded fringe. But even though she rolled up the sleeves the blouse was too big.

"But not nearly as big as one of Cade's shirts."

With a sigh she turned back to the box which also held a pair of faded jeans with a tear near the hem. The jeans were a surprisingly good fit except for the length. Cade had said Bonita was tall. He hadn't mentioned that she must have had a figure to die for.

Near the bottom of the box was a pair of fancy boots, badly scuffed and scarred by a series of teeth marks. At a guess, a dog had enjoyed several hours of play with the dirty, white-fringed boots. They were good leather and only half a size larger than she normally wore.

A picture fell out of one of the boots. Picking it up, Jayne found herself looking at a strikingly beautiful woman with a mass of thick dark hair and a figure to kill for. Bonita. Beside her stood a boy who was too old to be her son, though he looked so much like her it was amazing.

Jayne sighed, understanding why Cade was only mildly attracted to her. Not that she wanted him to be attracted, despite the racy dream she'd had just before waking. At least her fantasy life was a lot more interesting since meeting Cade McGovern, but that was all it would ever be. Cade had made his lack of intentions completely clear where she was concerned. Jayne put the picture back in the box.

Garments in hand, she put pillows on either side of the baby so Heather couldn't go anywhere, and headed for the bathroom. Cade would be annoyed, but Jayne was taking a shower.

Washing her hair was tricky, and Cade's supplies didn't run to things like cream rinse or a hair dryer. Fortunately, he did have a comb. Feeling clean for the first time in days was worth everything.

She was still working through the snarls in her hair one-handed when Cade called through the door.

"Come in. Your timing is good. Would you cut the pant legs…?" One look at his face sent her stomach plunging. "What's wrong?"

"Someone got to the SUV. They sliced all the tires including the spare."

Suddenly, it was hard to breathe. "When?"

"Good question."

He took in her outfit with enigmatic eyes and she tried not to feel like a pretend cowgirl or the child he thought she was, playing dress up.

"Are we trapped here now?"

"No. We've got horses. Rio's saddling one now." He took the scissors from the sink, bent and cut away the excess fabric with quick sure movements. "Rio's going for Hap to bring the truck back." He set the scissors on the sink and pulled a gun from his pocket. "I already know you can handle a rifle. Can you handle a .38?"

Her stomach gave a lurch. "Same principle," she managed to say calmly. "Point and fire."

"That'll work. Here. Keep this on you."

She took the heavy metal with an even heavier heart. "Is this necessary?"

"We were patrolling outside off and on all night, yet someone came right up to the house while we were inside."

"If the person wanted to hurt us why didn't he?"

Cade rubbed his chin with the back of his hand, then pushed up the brim of his hat with the knuckle of his index finger.

"He's toying with us. I can only think of a few reasons for someone to want to isolate us like this. None of them are good. Stay with Heather and away from windows. Zed and I are going to do a thorough search."

"You don't think Zed…?"

He shook his head but his shoulders slumped. Despite clean clothing and a freshly shaven jaw that made him look younger and sexier than ever, Cade looked so tired she longed to reach out and hug him.

"I think it's my ex-brother-in-law. Luís idolized his older sister, and he blames me for her death."

"I don't understand. You said she ran off with another man."

"Luís doesn't know that. He thinks she left me because I didn't treat her well. He may be trying to punish me for her death. So far, the only problems have had nuisance value. But the way things are escalating, it's possible…''

''What?''

His gray eyes darkened to smoke beneath the brim of his hat.

''Luís may think you're his sister's replacement. That may have pushed him over some edge. I don't know. I didn't think he was rabid, but I may have judged wrong. He could be more dangerous than I credited.''

''You said he was just a kid.''

''He'd be seventeen by now.'' Cade sighed and pulled his hat back down low over his eyes. ''I don't want anyone getting seriously hurt.''

Cade had kept the truth from a young boy who idolized his sister. It's what she would have expected from a man like him.

''I should have sold this place to Hap after my grandfather died, and headed up to Colorado like I'd planned,'' Cade said more to himself than to her.

''You're just tired.''

Offering comfort, she laid a hand on his arm. It was a mistake. Touching him was a definite mistake.

A curious tremor ran through her body and it wasn't from the weakness she'd felt earlier. This was more like anticipation. She'd always had boyfriends. But Cade was no boy. Kissing those hard firm lips would be very different from any of the people she had ever dated. She knew it with a certainty that went bone deep.

Cade looked down at her hand on his bare arm. Dark-gray eyes stared into hers sending a new jolt of sensation deep in her belly.

''I am tired,'' he said softly. ''Too tired for games.''

Her heart beat much too fast. Her mouth went dry. She couldn't seem to tear her gaze from his.

"I don't know what you mean."

Rough hard hands snaked out to clasp either side of her head. His fingers threaded her damp hair and his mouth covered hers in a kiss of masculine possession that she felt in every pore of her body. The wildly exhilarating sensation transcended pain and drugs and fear, leaving room for nothing except the devastating possession of his lips on hers.

Emotions rioted in her body. Coherent thought was impossible. Incredible longing swept her as he deepened the kiss to a level more intimate than any she had ever experienced. This wasn't the casual touch of tongues. This was a mating.

His hand covered her breast, kneading gently. Living currents of excitement had her melting into that kiss, pressing against him, urging him on with small sounds she'd never known she was capable of. She didn't want him to ever stop.

He drew back without warning. His rough hands had to steady her to keep her from collapsing.

"Stay with Heather," he said gruffly. "I'll be back in a few minutes to change your bandage."

Speechless, Jayne stumbled into the bedroom to collapse on the edge of the bed. It was just a kiss.

Sure. And Texas was just a state.

She could not—would not—fall in love with Cade McGovern. He'd shatter her heart as surely as his wife had shattered his.

Yet she wanted Cade in a physical and emotional way that she had never wanted anyone else in her life. A sound that was part laugh, part sob broke past lips that still tingled from his kiss. She had to get out of here. Her father and brothers would be horrified. She was falling in love with a cowboy.

She forced her mind away from the man and the kiss that had left her emotions in turmoil and tried to focus. Someone had slashed the SUV's tires. The incident may have nothing to do with her, but the baby ring was out there somewhere, just waiting for her to surface again. Her family might be worried sick by now. And a small part of her was terrified that the bullet had done some sort of permanent damage.

But none of those reasons were as compelling as her main one. She needed to leave before Cade got so far under her skin it would take a surgical knife to remove him.

"I need a sling or a backpack or something that will let me carry you and leave my hands free," she told the baby. Talking to the infant soothed her rattled mind. "Cade doesn't want me. He just…"

Just what? Was looking for a diversion? Was overwhelmed by sudden passion seeing her in his wife's old clothing?

She stared around the room until her gaze fell on the box and a large woven shawl with an ominous dark stain in one corner. She sniffed the material, but there was no scent to tell her what had caused the stain. Forcing her mind from Cade she experimented until she fashioned a sling of sorts, knotting it together as tightly as she could.

Sitting on the bed, she put the makeshift sling over her head and secured the baby inside. It took a bit of maneuvering, but finally Heather rested against Jayne's chest. It wasn't pretty, it wasn't comfortable, but if it was needed, it would do the trick, at least for a little while.

Despite Cade's order, Jayne walked to the bedroom window and gazed outside. She could see the edge of the barn and the corral clearly from here. Rio was stuffing a couple of bottles of water into a pair of saddlebags. A large dappled horse shifted restlessly beside him waiting to be saddled.

"Good idea. We'd better repack your diaper bag, Heather."

Jayne was doing exactly that when a shadow fell on the back door. She spun around, sending knives of pain down her arm. Her good hand reached for the heavy weight of the gun in her pocket, but the door flew open before she could bring it out. Cade stepped inside, stopping when he saw her.

Something hot and sensual came and went in his hard expression before he could hide his gaze by lowering his eyes beneath the brim of his hat.

"What's this?" he asked, indicating the baby and the shawl and the diaper bag.

"An experiment," she replied, pleased that her voice came out without any of the quivering that raged inside her. "I was getting things ready to go. Carrying her like this leaves my hands free. But this isn't particularly comfortable, so if you don't mind putting her back in her car seat for me…?"

Cade lifted Heather from the makeshift sling. His hand brushed Jayne's breast. Their gazes locked for a heartbeat out of time.

"I'm sorry."

And Jayne didn't know if the words were for that accidental touch or what had happened between them earlier. Her nipples tingled right along with the rest of her.

He strapped Heather into her car seat.

"Did you find anything outside?"

She couldn't believe her voice sounded so normal.

"Nothing."

"So now what?"

"Now we change your bandage."

Panic clawed at her stomach. "That isn't necessary."

"You must have gotten it wet when you showered."

"Not too badly. It'll dry."

"You're skin is still warm, Jayne. I may need to lance the wound."

"You'll have to show me a medical degree first."

His lips curved gently. "Have a seat while I look at it."

She would have to unbutton her blouse. He would have to touch her. Jayne took a long shuddering breath. She could handle this—because she had to. The bandages were wet and she couldn't change them herself.

"You'll have to take the blouse off," he said, returning with a small blue bag and setting his hat on the table.

Her saliva went into hiding. Did he have to look so incredibly sensual? Jayne shook her head.

"Jayne—"

"I'm not wearing a bra."

The very air sizzled. His lips parted and his gray eyes turned a fascinating shade of silver. She battled the temptation to reach out and touch the strand of dark hair falling against his forehead. He lowered his gaze but not before she glimpsed the rapid beat of the pulse in his neck.

"Unbutton it so I can pull the bandage off your shoulder," he said levelly.

Her fingers fumbled with the buttons. Panic hovered at the edges of her mind, but it was a panic mixed with a thrill of excitement. Whether it was the clothing or her looks, Cade wanted her with the same intensity she wanted him.

"You'll have to undo another button."

For a second her heart paused, before racing wildly. Her gaze had found the zipper on his tight-fitting jeans and the very noticeable bulge they contained. Somehow, that reassured her. Her confidence returned. Her brothers had taught her the best defense was a strong offense.

"Angling for a quick peek?"

Red stained his neck. "Are you deliberately trying to provoke me?"

"I didn't know I could."

"Oh, yeah. You knew."

She couldn't think of a response as he lowered the shirt off her shoulder. His touch was gentle, impersonal, as he peeled away the tape. But he was still aroused.

"H-how's it look?"

"Not too bad, considering."

"Considering what? That I have a hole in my shoulder? That my arm's going to fall off? What?"

She turned her head and decided he was right. A scab covered the area. The wound still looked nasty, but not as inflamed as it had yesterday. She'd have a scar, but that would have happened even if she'd had immediate access to a hospital and doctors.

"You were lucky, you know," Cade said. "I'm pretty sure the bullet either missed the bone completely or just nicked it slightly. I don't think any real damage was done."

"If I'd been lucky, the bullet would have missed my shoulder completely."

His lips curved in a definite smile.

"You should do that more often."

Instantly, his smile faded and he busied himself with the first-aid supplies.

"What was she like?" Jayne wished she could bite back the words the moment they were uttered.

"Who?"

There was nothing to do but finish the question. "Your wife."

"What difference does—"

"Did you love her?"

Cade drew back with a scowl.

"It's not idle curiosity, Cade. I admit there's some of that," she added honestly. "But if her brother is a threat I'd like to understand the situation."

Cade began retaping the wound. "You're in more danger from your husband than you are from Luís."

"That isn't an answer."

"My private life isn't up for display."

"So you did love her."

"No." He glared at her. "I wanted her. Just like I want you. Right here. Right now."

Jayne couldn't seem to breathe. Her entire body tingled with wild longing.

"But I've learned a few things since then. Bonita had a hot body and a smile that could turn a man hard in an instant. All the men wanted her."

Just like I want you. Right here. Right now.

She was still reeling from the impact of those words and the desire they'd unleashed.

"Bonita followed the circuit and the cowboys," Cade said evenly. "Zed introduced her to me one night. They'd come into the bar together, but she turned the full force of her attention on me. I gathered the two of them had had a fight. Zed up and left her there after a few minutes."

"And you played the gentleman."

His jaw set. "Bonita wasn't looking for a gentleman. I gave her what she was looking for."

His crude words were punishment, Jayne realized. He finished with her shoulder and turned away. She began buttoning her blouse.

"Is that why you married her?"

"You aren't going to let it drop, are you?"

"I told you—"

"Fine, you want the truth? We got drunk one night in Las Vegas. I'm not real clear on the details, but in the morning we woke up in a cheap motel with several thousand dollars in cash including two hundred dollars in quarters, a king-size hangover and a marriage neither of us wanted."

His clipped words and pained expression made her sorry she'd asked.

"We decided what the heck. Marriage didn't seem like such a bad idea. We got along okay and the sex was raw and hot. She looked great on my arm, and every guy on the circuit envied me."

He closed the blue case and stood rubbing the back of his neck. "My grandfather died a few weeks later and I inherited all this." He waved his hand to encompass the ranch at large. "Bonita was appalled to discover I would leave the exciting life of the rodeo circuit and move to the middle of nowhere to take up ranching. That wasn't in her plans."

"I'm sorry, Cade."

He didn't seem to hear or see her. He was lost in his bitter past.

"It had always been *my* plan. Hap offered to buy the Circle M from me when my grandfather died, but owning my own spread was my dream. It turned into a nightmare. Bonita was so unhappy that I turned the running of the spread over to Hap after a few months and agreed to return to the circuit. Only that wasn't enough for her, either. I could see it wasn't going to work for the long haul. We wanted different lives. I took a bad spill one day and went looking for my wife. She was turning her considerable charm on Zed in our hotel room.''

The keen edge of his pain reached her. Cade may not have loved her, but Bonita's betrayal, and especially the betrayal of a man he considered his friend, had cut his pride to the bone. As if reading her thoughts, he lifted his head and stared into her eyes.

''We came home that night. Three months later Bonita disappeared with a hired hand. By then I was glad. The only thing I felt when I heard she was dead was guilt—because I was relieved to have the whole thing over with.''

''I don't blame you.''

''Her brother does. I met him when I went to claim the body. I didn't even know she had a brother. Says a lot about my marriage, doesn't it?''

''It says a lot about Bonita.''

''Yeah. Well, Bonita had called Luís right before she left and told him I was abusive and cruel. He wanted to take out his grief and anger on me. I could have told him different, but what was the point?''

Her heart broke for the pain behind his words.

''I'm sorry.''

''Yeah? So am I, but life happens.''

The room filled with silence.

Finally she inhaled. She needed to speak the troubling thought that had formed.

"You said Bonita dated Zed first? What if he blames you for her death, too?"

Cade's body turned to stone. For a moment he didn't say anything.

"I thought you believed a man was innocent until proven guilty."

"I also believe in getting at the truth. Zed's here—on your ranch. He was at the line shack—with a horse. The phone lines may have been cut while he was sleeping in the bunkhouse. And he patrolled the yard last night when the tires could have been cut."

"His antibiotics may have saved your life," Cade pointed out.

"I appreciate that, but he has no beef with me. He knows I'm not Bonita's replacement. You said yourself the things that have been happening were more of a nuisance than a real threat."

"There isn't any way Zed could have gotten to the SUV Rio was driving."

"Are you sure?"

He stood there in silence. Finally, he let out a deep breath. "The sooner we get you off this ranch the better," he said finally. "Tell me why your husband shot you in the back."

Eyes of gray granite seemed to penetrate her soul.

"He wasn't my husband," she told him honestly.

"You want to tell me—"

He spun with a speed that startled a gasp out of her as someone raced up to the back door. Rio burst inside and came to a quick halt when he found himself facing down a revolver that looked like the twin to the one Cade had given her.

"I thought you left," Cade said, lowering the gun.

"Yeah. I mean, no. That is, I was about to leave

when the stupid horse got spooked by one of the barn cats. He cut his left hind pretty good on a piece of fencing. Zed helped me get him calmed down, but he thinks the horse needs stitches. You'd better come have a look while I saddle Twister.''

Cade muttered something under his breath. ''I'll be right back,'' he told her.

''Can I help?'' Jayne asked.

''Yeah. Wait here and stay out of trouble.'' He moved through the door before she could protest.

HEATHER WAS FED and changed and Cade hadn't returned. Jayne paced the floor, increasingly restless. The day was slipping away. Had the horse really been spooked by a barn cat or had someone given him a scare?

Her brain locked in stark fear as someone slunk past the kitchen window.

Despite the thudding of her heart, Jayne raced to the kitchen, but the man was out of sight. She'd only caught the flash of a light-colored Stetson. Cade, Zed and Rio wouldn't be sneaking around the house like that. It had to be whoever was causing Cade all the trouble.

She didn't remember drawing the gun he'd given her, but its weight filled her hand. She ran to the living room to shout for Cade and her world came to a crashing halt.

A dark-colored sedan sat in front of the house. Cade and Zed stood talking with the two occupants. The men still wore the same ill-fitting suits, the same red ties.

The baby ring had found her.

She should have told Cade the truth. There was no telling what sort of story they were spinning right now, but Cade would have no reason to disbelieve whatever they told him.

In fact, the way Zed was holding the rifle so casually at his side, it occurred to her again that he might be working with them. What did she know about Zed, really?

Come to that, what did she know about Cade? While she was certain he wasn't part of the baby ring, he'd made it clear he wanted to get rid of her. The kidnappers had driven right up to his front door to make that chore easy for him. Her only chance was to reach the barn and one of the horses. The low-slung car couldn't follow her if she headed across the field toward the hills.

Jayne snatched up the sling, placed the sleeping baby inside and grabbed the diaper bag. Carefully, she opened the back door, her eyes scanning for the other person she'd seen.

Nothing moved.

Taking a deep breath, she ran for the barn, waiting for the shout of discovery, or the cold impact of a bullet in her back. Neither happened. A saddled horse stood tethered just inside the barn. Big and black, he eyed her approach. This had to be the horse Rio was saddling to replace the injured animal. She recognized the saddle-bags, already on his back.

"Hey there, Twister."

Fear choked her voice, but she tried to sound calm, knowing the horse would pick up on her fear. If he was skittish, she'd never be able to mount.

The horse twitched an ear in her direction and whuffled, switching away a bothersome fly with his tail.

"Good boy, Twister."

Though everything inside her urged her to hurry, she approached slowly, letting the animal know exactly where she was at all times. She spoke quietly as she patted his neck and stroked him gently. Despite his name, Twister remained placid, while she went around to his side and hung the diaper bag over the roping horn.

She checked the cinch, adjusted the stirrups for her shorter legs, and undid the lead line. All the while she crooned softly to the animal as fear beat a tattoo inside her chest. A mounting block stood against the barn wall. Looping the lead line over the horn, she gathered the reins and used the mounting block to step onto the horse. Twister barely acknowledged the additional weight.

Her shoulder screamed in pain when she jarred it, but she ignored the injury, settling the baby against her chest so Heather rested along her damaged side. That left her right hand free. Like the well-trained horse he appeared to be, Twister responded immediately to the slight pressure of the rein and her heels. She wasn't surprised. A man like Cade would have dependable stock.

She guided Twister toward the opening at the far end of the barn, the familiar scents and sounds making her suddenly homesick for her parents' ranch. Keeping the barn between herself and the men, she broke into a gentle lope. Twister had an easy stride and the flopping bag and the strange weight on his back didn't seem to disturb him at all.

If only she had some knowledge of the local geography. Was she heading toward a neighbor or away from potential help? She reined in her desire to gallop full out and headed in a straight line for the distant foothills. She would protect this child at all costs.

Chapter Eight

Cade heard Heather begin to cry as the door slammed shut behind him. He'd been certain he could control his emotions, but his normally cool restraint faded like so much mist every time he got near Jayne. He wanted her. And he hated that she knew what a fool he'd been over Bonita.

Was he fated to keep making the same mistakes over and over again?

No, Jayne might be dressed in Bonita's clothing, but she was nothing at all like his former wife. She was nothing like anyone he'd ever known. She maddened him, fascinated him and made him dream impossible things. But kissing her had been the dumbest thing he'd done in a long time.

He was a loner. He liked his life that way. There was safety in being a loner. Only the cows knew when he was out of sorts and they didn't care. He wasn't giving up his freedom or his ranch again for any woman—and women and ranching didn't mix. Besides, babies were messy, bothersome creatures who grew up into kids. He refused to think about how good it felt holding the infant, knowing she trusted him to care for her. Heather was special, but she'd grow into a child and God knew, he didn't have any experience with kids. Especially little girls. A kid would probably hate ranch life.

But he hadn't.

Not even when his parents were alive and he lived with them on his dad's small spread in Colorado. And why was he even thinking about this? Just more proof of how twisted his thoughts had become.

As he and Rio and Zed worked on the fractious horse, all sorts of crazy thoughts lingered in his mind. Overriding everything was the knowledge that he needed to get Jayne off his ranch and out of his life before it was too late.

Too late for what?

He watched as Rio saddled Twister.

"Company comin'," Zed said quietly and reached for the rifle.

A dark sedan car came bouncing up the long road to the ranch house. Cade was surprised the vehicle hadn't bottomed out.

"City type. Probably lost," Cade muttered. "Nobody I know."

"More trouble?" Rio asked coming to stand beside the two men inside the open barn door.

"Or it could be help," Zed suggested.

"Let's hope for that and prepare for the other," Cade decided. "Rio, take a flanking position on the far side of the house. Don't let the driver or his passenger see you. If trouble happens, get Jayne and the baby out the back door. Your job is to keep them safe at all costs. Zed, take the rifle out in the pasture—"

"Don't you think it might be more effective for me to walk up behind you carrying the rifle?" Zed asked.

Trust Zed with a rifle at his back?

"Rio, go."

He measured Zed with a quelling look. Zed didn't even flinch under that stare. He waited with his usual laconic patience for Cade's decision.

"All right," Cade agreed. "Keep the rifle handy and let's go see if these city folks have a cell phone we can use."

They claimed they didn't, but Cade's instincts began clamoring even before the two men introduced themselves as FBI agents flashing badges and credentials so fast his eyes didn't have time to take them in.

"We're looking for a young girl and a baby," the burly spokesman announced. "She's got long blond hair, skinny, about five feet tall. She was wearing a white blouse and dark pants when she kidnapped the baby from a supermarket parking lot. The infant is only five days old."

Cade's gut knotted painfully. "Kidnapped?"

The two heads bobbed in tandem.

"Why would you look for them way out here?" Cade asked without glancing at Zed to see how he was taking this information.

"We traced the license plate on your black pickup truck after we found this in the back."

He dangled a single crystal earring.

"We think that maybe the girl wore earrings like these," the other agent added.

Cade had promised Jayne his protection, but if she'd kidnapped the baby…

"Isn't the black pickup the one that got stolen, Cade?" Zed asked stepping forward. His expression was as neutral as his tone of voice, but he studied the newcomers alertly.

"Yeah," Cade agreed, making a split second decision. "I picked up some supplies three days ago and when I parked the truck and started unloading, someone stole it. I figured it was a drifter who happened by and seized the opportunity. You say you found it in town?''

One of the men nodded while the other cursed. ''Musta been her,'' the shorter man said. ''She probably waited for her chance and took off.''

The spokesman scratched at his nose, his brow furrowed in thought. ''We'll have to go back to that bar and ask more questions. Someone must have seen her when she bailed.''

''Unless she stole another car,'' his companion blurted.

''Wouldn't that have been reported?'' Zed asked mildly.

The two agents looked momentarily disconcerted, but the spokesman recovered quickly. ''Yeah. Thanks for your help.''

''Do you want us to keep an eye out for her?''

''Not much point. She's probably long gone by now.''

They started to get back into their car.

''Hey, hold it. We still need some help out here,'' Cade told them. ''Someone cut our phone lines.''

They both stopped, half in and half out of the car.

''Yeah?''

''And they slashed the tires on the only vehicle I have left right now. We've also had fences cut, the herd spooked, a fire in the—''

Their interest immediately died.

''You'll have to report that to the local police. We can't—''

''That's what I want you to do!'' Cade said. ''If we could call the sheriff, we would.''

"Oh. Okay. We'll let someone know as soon as we get back to town."

"Maybe I could ride along with you," Zed suggested to Cade's surprise. "You can drop me at the sheriff's office."

"Sorry. We can't take you with us, but we'll let them know."

They scrambled back into their car, obviously anxious to be gone again. Raising another cloud of dust, they turned the sporty car around and bounced back the way they'd come.

"Did Jayne really kidnap that baby?" Rio asked, coming around the far side of the house.

Cade didn't bother to answer. Nor did he look at Zed. He could well imagine what his friend was thinking. Jayne had fooled him as completely as Bonita. Cade stared hard after the disappearing car before turning to stride toward the house and Jayne.

The second he stepped inside, he knew she was gone. The house felt empty and cold—like it had before Jayne had come to the Circle M.

The green-and-yellow baby bag was gone from the table, but the infant seat still sat there. Then he remembered the makeshift sling. She'd created that and packed the diaper bag before the men arrived. She'd been planning to run all along. The men were telling the truth.

Twister!

He spun around, nearly knocking Zed off his feet. "She's gone."

"Hold it a minute, Cade. You don't believe that bull they were spewing, do you?"

Did he? He didn't know. He only knew she was gone. He brushed past Zed, heading for the barn. Zed kept pace beside him.

"They had badges," Cade said tersely.

"So?"

Rio trotted along his other side, half running in an effort to keep pace with the two men.

"Didn't you find their behavior at all curious?" Zed demanded. "I sure did. Especially for FBI agents."

Cade reached the barn. Twister was gone. Even though he expected as much, the knowledge that she'd run sent a blade through his soul.

"You got something to say, spit it out, Zed," he snapped at the man's sympathetic expression.

"Okay. I know cops. Those two didn't act like cops. Anyone can buy a badge or fake credentials. You can get 'em off the Internet these days."

Cade thought about that for a heartbeat.

Zed pushed his point.

"Maybe Jayne's husband sent those two after her. If he saw you drive away that day they could be private investigators, or a pair of hired thugs," Zed insisted. "There's lots of explanations."

"Why does it matter to you?" he asked.

Zed's voice gentled. "I like her. She's got grit. And I think she's in real trouble."

"Yeah. You could call kidnapping real trouble."

Zed frowned.

"You may be right about those two, but either way, I have to find her."

"Want me to saddle Lafferty?" Zed offered.

"No. I'll take Aries and go after her myself. She'll have to travel slow with her shoulder and the baby. I need you and Rio to wait here for the sheriff."

Zed tipped his head with a skeptical expression. "Assuming the sheriff shows up, what do we tell him about Jayne?"

Cade cursed and reached for his tack. "Nothing. Don't say anything at all about her. Just report—no, you haven't been here long enough." He looked at Rio. The other cowboy wasn't the most capable on his ranch. Rio wouldn't be able to manage the conversation, either.

"Saddle Lafferty," he told Zed. "I need Hap to talk with the sheriff and explain what's been happening. Tell him to keep Jayne out of the conversation completely until I get back. Rio, keep a close watch on the horses and the buildings, all right?"

"Sure, Cade."

Aries snorted and stamped his foot as if sensing the tension in the air. Cade tossed the saddle over the horse's back while Zed reached for his own tack.

"I hope you know what you're doing, friend," Zed said softly.

Cade snorted. "Not likely. There's a woman involved."

Zed remained silent while Cade finished and swung into the saddle. At least this time the woman in question hadn't run off with one of his men.

"Cade?"

Zed's expression was creased by concern.

"Jayne isn't Bonita."

"What's that supposed to mean?"

"I don't trust those men."

"Meaning you do trust Jayne?"

"Meanin' I'd give her a chance to explain before I jumped down her throat. You tend to hit first and skip the questions altogether."

"I've never struck a woman in my life!"

Zed rubbed his jaw and Cade knew they were both remembering the day Cade found Zed and Bonita together in the motel room.

''Just listen to what she has to say before you make up your mind about what's going on.''

It had only been a matter of hours that Jayne had been telling him much the same thing about Zed. ''How chummy did you two get last night?'' Cade demanded.

Zed's features tightened, then relaxed into a sad expression. ''Sometimes I think you're dumber than mud.'' He rechecked the cinch on Lafferty before swinging into the saddle. ''I'll find Hap.''

''Do that,'' Cade snapped, puzzled by Zed's cryptic words. He turned his thoughts from the cowboy to Jayne. She wouldn't have wanted to be seen when she left. That meant she headed across the pasture toward the thicket near the base of the foothills. Cade was no tracker, but he didn't figure she could be all that far ahead of him. He urged Aries forward, scanning the surrounding terrain.

Had she run because of the men? Or had she run because of the kiss they'd shared? Was she afraid Cade couldn't control his passion? Neither she nor Zed seemed to think Cade could control his other base emotions, either. Okay, he did tend to have a hot temper, Cade acknowledged, but it generally cooled just as quickly as it heated up.

He automatically started toward his neighbor's ranch. Belatedly, it occurred to him that Jayne wouldn't know the direction of the nearest spread. She'd either head up into the foothills or go in the other direction. With the baby and her shoulder, he doubted she'd try riding uphill.

A few minutes later he heard the sound of a baby crying. He urged Aries forward until he practically rode right up on top of them. Jayne sat on the ground holding the baby, feeding it a bottle. Twister stood nearby investigating a clump of grass.

"Are you hurt? Were you thrown?" He swung down, alarmed.

"Of course I wasn't thrown." She seemed unfazed to see him. "Heather was hungry and I made the mistake of stopping to change her and get a fresh bottle. Then I realized I couldn't remount while I'm holding her without a rock or something to stand on. Stupid shoulder."

Tension drained from his body. He swung down from the saddle. "We had visitors. They say you kidnapped the baby."

"And you believed them?"

So, she had seen the men.

"Frankly, I don't know what to believe."

"They're lying."

He hardened his heart. "They had badges, Jayne. FBI identification."

"Fake."

Her calm certainty rattled him.

"Talk to me. Tell me what's going on here."

"I tried to tell you. You didn't want to listen."

"This is no time to be stubborn." Cade held on to his temper. "I'll listen now," he said softly.

If she knew how close he was to the breaking point, she gave no sign. Instead, she brushed back strands of spun-gold hair from her face, instantly diverting his attention. She looked young and beautiful and terribly innocent.

"I'm a private investigator."

"What?"

How could she say something like that with a straight

face? Did she think he was a total idiot? Of course she did. Hell, maybe she was right.

"I had a lead on a black-market baby ring," she continued, blithely unaware of his internal reaction. "They make the exchange in shopping centers. Heather was about to be sold when something went wrong. They pulled guns so I tried to get her away, but they came after me. I escaped, only the car ran out of gas. I had to walk until I stumbled on your town. Unfortunately, the man in the silver car was there ahead of me. He was talking on the phone on the far side of the gas station. That's why I hid in the back of your truck. The rest you know."

A rush of anger mingled with a wave of hurt that she would lie to him so blatantly after he'd essentially saved her life. "And you expect me to stand here and believe a story like that?"

"It's the truth!" Her jaw set in familiar mutinous lines.

The story was so ridiculous he couldn't believe she even made such a feeble attempt. Did she really think he'd be that gullible?

Of course she did. He'd told her about Bonita. She probably thought he had sap stenciled on his forehead. The worst of it was that despite her lie, part of him did want to protect her no matter what the truth. But the sane part wanted to shake her until she coughed up some honest answers. He hooked his thumbs in his waistband. He didn't trust himself to touch her in that moment.

"Give me the baby."

She blinked in obvious surprise. "Why? What are you going to do?"

The protective way she clutched the infant hardened

his jaw and his resolve. Whatever the truth, he wasn't going to let her take the baby and ride out of here.

"You can't ride and carry her," he managed to say evenly.

"Of course I can. How do you think we got here? I just can't mount holding her without something to stand on."

"Give her here."

Her eyes widened. "You can't give her back to them! Don't you understand? They'll kill both of us and sell her to the highest bidder. They're part of an organized crime ring. Probably that one Governor Kincaid is going after so publicly. They can't afford to leave any witnesses behind."

He had to hand it to her, when she told a whopper, she made it big and bold. He reached down and lifted Heather from her arms. Jayne scrambled to her feet, grimacing slightly.

"What are you going to do?"

He eyed her calmly. "I'm going to take you both back to the ranch."

"I told you it isn't safe."

Her guileless expression meant nothing. Bonita used to have a similar look, especially when she was caught red-handed. When was he going to learn? Women learned to lie before they learned to speak.

"Do you have crystal earrings?" he demanded.

"Do I what?"

"Have some crystal earrings?"

Her hand went to her naked earlobes, fingering them in puzzlement. "I did, but I lost them. What does that have to do with anything?"

"Those men found one in the back of my truck."

Her eyes widened in stark fear. Whatever the truth really was, she was terrified of those two men.

"Then they know I'm here! We've got to go!"

He gripped her right arm with the hand that wasn't holding Heather. "Calm down. I told them the truck was stolen. They think you took it."

The panic began to fade from her eyes. "Then let's go! They won't be fooled for long."

"I'll give you a leg up."

"I can do it as long as you hold Heather."

She hurried over to Twister, but Cade was pleased to see she slowed down when she reached him. She knew how to approach a horse. Twister gave her an indifferent look when she took up the reins and mounted with only minor difficulty.

"Arm okay?"

"I'm fine. Give me the baby."

"I'll carry her."

"I'd rather hold her myself."

Sure, and then she'd take off.

"I don't think so." He walked over to Aries, gave the horse a pat and swung into the saddle. "We're going back to the ranch."

"We can't! I just told you—"

"I know what you told me and I know what they told me. And I'm real tired of being caught in the middle here." Jayne flinched and he hardened his heart against her look of betrayal. "I asked the agents to tell the sheriff about the cut phone lines and the problems we're having."

"They can't afford to go near the sheriff! They're no more FBI than I am. We have to ride to the nearest telephone. You can call the sheriff from there."

"No."

"But—"

"Jayne, no matter who those guys were, odds are they're going to canvass my neighbors just to be sure you aren't hiding nearby. I've got good neighbors. They mind their own business. But they're law-abiding, churchgoing people. They aren't going to cover for you. If they see you with me, they'll tell those guys you're here."

"I don't want anyone to—"

"When they flash those badges, my neighbors will do whatever is necessary to keep trouble from their door. And you can't blame them."

"I wouldn't. But—"

"If those men are federal agents like they claim, they'll let the sheriff know we need help out here. Sheriff Beaufort will ride out and you can tell him your story."

"And if I'm telling the truth and those phony agents don't send the sheriff out?" she demanded.

"Then we'll drive into town first thing in the morning."

"Why not tonight?"

Obviously, she couldn't wait to see the last of him. He was the one who should be feeling that way.

"You're in no shape to ride that far. There's a red stain on your shirt which means you opened that wound again."

Jayne spared a glance at her shoulder where a tiny red spot was visible against the blue of the blouse.

"I sent Zed for Hap and the truck," he continued. "By the time they make it back here it'll be too late to go into town."

"Why? Does your sheriff only work from eight to five?"

Cade sighed, holding on to his temper with supreme effort. "By the time we get into town and talk to the sheriff, it'll be too late for me to pick up the new tires, get the wires fixed on the radio and get back here before dark. And I am not making a third run into Darwin this week. In case it escaped your notice, I'm trying to run a working ranch out here. I know you can't wait to get away from me, but don't worry, I promise I won't touch you again after I check your shoulder."

"What do you mean?"

"That kiss won't happen again. If you want, I can get Zed to change your bandage."

The saddle creaked as she leaned forward and stared at him. "Why would I want Zed to change my bandage? What are you talking about?"

"You were packing to leave long before those men showed up," Cade said. "I realize my kiss scared you off, and I'm sor—"

Her mouth dropped open in such an expression of shock that Cade stopped in the middle of his apology. He had the bad feeling he'd not only miscalculated, but that he'd just made an utter fool of himself as well.

"You...I... Oh! How could I have thought you were...? You've got an ego the size of your spread, do you know that? You think I left because of a simple kiss?"

Outrage filled her voice and added color to her cheeks.

She'd thought that kiss was simple? It had seared its way into his memory.

"You are such a...an arrogant male! I wanted to be ready to go in a hurry in case there was more trouble. I *left* because the baby-nappers were out front and someone was sneaking around the back of the house!"

"Sneaking around the house? Oh. You must have seen Rio when I sent him to cover us."

She made everything sound so believable. All except the part about her being a private investigator and saving the infant from a baby ring, of course.

Unless it was her baby.

The thought rooted, making the first real sense he'd gleaned from any of this. An unwanted pregnancy, a hasty decision to give up the child, a change of heart, a stolen baby—that scenario he could buy into.

"The guy that shot you wasn't your husband, was he?" Cade asked.

"I told you I wasn't married!"

"Was he the baby's father?"

She hesitated, and it was that momentary hesitation that convinced him he was right. She was still protecting the bastard.

"The man who approached you at that store was working with the kidnappers," she said quickly, bringing Twister to a stop. "Please, Cade, you have to trust me. Going back to the ranch is a bad idea. What if they're watching? What if they come back?"

"We'll deal with that if and when it happens."

She shook her head. "I can't take that chance."

"You don't have a choice."

"Yes, I do. Give me Heather. I'll ride to the nearest telephone."

"Who do you plan to call?"

"My brother!"

Instantly, he thought of Luís. How was it, Cade wondered, that he kept getting tangled up with women who had brothers? Or was she making up the brother in hopes he'd let her go?

"What really happened, Jayne? Did you change your mind after you gave Heather up for adoption?"

Her mouth opened and snapped shut again. Hurt glimmered in her eyes, but she covered it with sarcastic anger. "You have it all figured out, don't you?"

"No," he admitted feeling suddenly tired. "That's why I want you to tell me the truth."

"You don't recognize the truth when you hear it. Go back to your ranch and your cows. You have enough problems of your own. I'll handle Heather and my situation from here on out. Now give me Heather!"

Grit and determination lent authority to her voice, but the slow spread of the red stain belied her ability to do carry out her plan.

"You can't even sit a saddle without starting the bleeding up again. How far do you think you're going to get?"

She spared the stain a brief glance. "As far as I need to. Hand me the baby."

"When we reach the house."

Impotent with rage, she glared at him as he spurred Aries forward.

"Your ranch is such a safe place for us to go," she called after him. "I feel real secure with people walking right up to the house and slashing tires while I'm sleeping."

Her angry thrust found its intended target. Cade set his teeth and kept riding.

"I give you my word I'll keep you and the baby safe," he said without looking back.

A breeze rustled the treetops, drawing both their gazes skyward. Low dark clouds scudded across the horizon. Cade reined up and nodded in their direction.

"Now unless you want to take a chance on getting

soaked in addition to lost out here with limited supplies, we need to get back to the ranch now.''

Jayne's eyes closed in sudden defeat. All the energy seemed to leave her body in a single breath.

"Come on,'' he urged gently. "We can beat the storm back.''

Jayne didn't say a word, not even when he kicked Aries into a canter. He knew she followed. He also knew that while the sky looked menacing, they weren't likely to actually be rained on any time soon. But the threat had not only effectively silenced Jayne, it got her moving again in the right direction.

Rio met them at the barn with the news that no one had returned to the ranch—not even Zed and Hap. Rio offered to see to the horses while Cade took Heather into the house. Jayne led the way without speaking.

"Let me put Heather down and I'll look at your shoulder.''

"That won't be necessary.''

"It's bleeding, Jayne.''

"I'll take care of it.''

"Not unless you're a contortionist.''

She glared at him but stopped arguing and began unbuttoning the blouse. Cade went for the first-aid supplies, making a mental note to replenish the cache when he got to Darwin Crossing.

Jayne went into the bedroom and sat on the side of the bed. A slight tremor when he touched her was her only reaction to his presence. Cade removed the bandage and studied her shoulder. The scab had opened, but it was already reforming and the bleeding had stopped. He applied more rubbing alcohol over the area.

"Ow!''

"Sorry.''

"Yeah, right." She glared at him while he covered the wound with a piece of gauze and began taping it once again. Bending over her this way gave him an unexpected view straight down her open blouse.

Her breasts were high and firm with rosy tips that began to bud as he stared. They would fit perfectly in his hands.

He tore his gaze away, but not before she caught him looking. Shame sent heat up his neck.

"Sorry," he muttered.

"Did you get a good look?" she asked scathingly.

Cade closed his eyes and counted to ten. When he opened them, she'd made no move to rebutton the blouse.

"You'll want to lie down," he said evenly. "I'll help you get your boots off."

Her head tipped to one side, the spill of silken hair covering part of the blouse's opening, adding to the sensual image she presented. She could arouse him without even trying. It was maddening.

Her anger seemed to melt away. "Do you always send such mixed messages?"

"Jayne—"

"One minute you act like you want to take me to bed. The next, you act like you can't wait to get rid of me."

She was right. That was exactly how he'd been acting. Because that was how he was feeling. He flexed his fingers to keep them at his sides and away from the temptation of her hair.

"See, that's exactly what I'm talking about."

"What?" he demanded.

"The way you were just looking at me."

"How was I looking at you?"

"The way a man looks…at a lover."

The room fell so silent Cade could hear his heart beating.

"Like the way you're looking at me, right now?" he asked.

Her expression didn't falter.

"Probably."

"Talk about running hot and cold, one minute you're running from me, the next you're inviting more than you realize."

"I was running from the kidnappers, not you. And what makes you think I don't know what I'm doing? You're the one who can't decide what he wants."

"Oh, I know, all right. I want you," he told her through clenched teeth. "I just don't want to want you."

Her lips parted and she blinked in surprise, but her recovery was swift.

"That clears everything up nicely."

"You're too young and—"

She stood so fast he took a step back. Anger blazed in her eyes.

"I am a twenty-four-year-old adult woman. I can't help it if I look younger than I really am. They say in ten years I'll be thrilled with that fact. Right now it's a royal pain in the butt. Try getting anyone to take you seriously when you look like this. I am quite capable of making my own decisions. And quite capable of taking care of myself."

He wanted to smile, but he remembered the seriousness of the situation.

"I can see how good you are at that last part." Her blouse hung open providing him with a view that would surprise her. Despite his determination not to be attracted to her, the tempting sight stirred a very basic reaction.

"So what do you want from me, Jayne? This?"

Before he could think, he pulled her into his arms and covered her mouth with his own.

Chapter Nine

Jayne was drowning in sensations. Nothing had prepared her for the overpowering onslaught of such a highly charged sensual attack. His hand spanned the back of her head. His fingers threaded her hair, holding her head in possessive demand while his lips and tongue plundered her mouth.

This was what it was like to be claimed, she thought in stunned elation. And then thinking became impossible as her own desire caught fire and she sought to return the kiss with demands of her own.

Her body strained upward, trying to draw his tall strength down against her more fully. Her good arm circled his neck. The hard, raw hunger of his body stirred hers to an answering excitement. Tiny sounds of gratification caught in the back of her throat as his hand sought the shape of her breast beneath the blouse.

Cade groaned when her fingers brushed the zipper on his pants, lightly tracing the outline pressed so boldly there. His hands shaped her body, clutching her bottom in blatant sexual heat.

A shiver of liquid desire made her weak and heady with pleasure. Her body responded to the incredible sensations, hungering for more. No one had ever aroused her to this point.

Because no one else had been Cade.

She didn't know her blouse was unbuttoned until his mouth covered the pointed thrust of her breast. The intimacy was bold, shocking—exhilarating.

"Cade!"

She clutched his head, her fingers lost in his hair. He gazed at her, his eyes as dark as a stormy sky and burnished by passion.

"Do you want me to stop?"

Never.

Images of Cade—tenderly caring for the baby, protectively standing guard over them at the cabin, fiercely struggling to protect his land and his men, yet unwilling to see a young man suffer for his foolish acts—rolled together in her thoughts. Oh, yes, she wanted him. Shocked, she realized he was the only man she had ever met that she did want.

"Don't you dare stop!"

His grin was crooked but pleased, yet still he hesitated. She could see the debate going on inside him. And offered him her own smile.

"I really am twenty-four."

His eyes gleamed in satisfaction. "You'd better be."

His lips claimed her mouth once more, but this time his kiss softened, even as his body tightened against hers. The kiss became a tender, sensual exploration that pushed aside the world, narrowing her focus to him. To them. She forgot the stabbing pain of her shoulder, forgot all the reasons she shouldn't be doing this, and gave herself up to the heady sensations Cade was creating.

He undressed her slowly, careful not to jar her shoulder. She had never been nude in front of a man in her life, but this felt so right she didn't have a moment of hesitation. His gaze made her feel beautiful and exquisitely alive. She reached for the buttons on his shirt. He let her undo them one by one, pausing to kiss his mouth and his chest between each button. He made an approving noise as she finished, but when she reached for his zipper he shook his head.

"I'll do it. You take too long."

"Yes." Her voice was as shaky as her body. "Hurry."

She lay back on the bed and watched him yank off his boots and socks and slide his jeans and briefs down over his hard, muscular thighs. They weren't the only things that were hard and muscular. Her body went hot then cold at the sight of him, fully aroused. For the first time, she considered the step she was about to take.

"Don't worry," he said, opening the nightstand drawer. "I have protection. I wouldn't put you at risk."

Her heart thundered in her chest. Protection. Only now did it occur to her that if they continued, pregnancy was a possible outcome.

A baby of her own. One that she and Cade created. A little girl like Heather. A son, perhaps!

She reached out to touch him, but he shook his head. "Not this time. I'm too close. But you can slide this on for me, if you want."

Her hands trembled as she took the small sheath. The act was so intimate that he had to guide her hands while her stomach rioted in unleashed anticipation. He was so large. So incredibly smooth yet rigid.

He was breathing as hard as she was when she finished.

"I think, considering your shoulder, you'd better get on top," he said unsteadily.

"On top?"

His smile was purely masculine, definitely predatory. "Never done it that way?"

She shook her head. "I've never done it at all."

"It's like riding a horse. Only this saddle will fit you a whole lot tighter."

His hand cupped her breast and he bent to sample it with a long, drugging pull she felt to the core of her being.

Fear drained away, replaced by a need so strong, she automatically inched back on the bed to give him room. He watched her with transparent hunger, making her feel unbelievably sensual. Her heart pounded furiously, but the expression of blatant need in his eyes relaxed her trepidation. She quivered as his hands slid down the bare skin of her sides. She let him guide her into a position astride him, aware of him as she'd never been aware of anything in her life. Every nerve ending, every muscle, every part of her was vividly alive and aware of each new sensation.

"Cade?"

He pulled her head down to his waiting mouth and the kiss stole away her ability to think. His fingers investigated her body gently. A shiver coursed through her as he brushed the short, curling hairs to part her with exquisite tenderness. His eyes held her captive as he gently inserted first one finger and then two, cautiously stretching her. She couldn't prevent a soft intake of breath.

"I wouldn't have thought you'd be so tight," he said in husky approval. His eyes gleamed warmly as her body trembled on the brink of something incredible.

And when his thumb came to rest against a certain spot, she thought she was going to come apart in his hands. He lifted her in satisfaction, mindful of her shoulder, and lowered her onto his rigid staff. This time she inhaled sharply, knowing what was coming as he reached the membrane preventing his complete access.

"Jayne?" His eyes widened in shock.

She knew he was about to pull back, and she couldn't allow that. Not now. Not when she was so very close. She sank onto him, forcing him past the thin barrier, barely aware of a second of pain.

"Why? And why didn't you tell me?" he growled.

"I did. You didn't listen."

She tightened herself around him, the discomfort already fading to make room for this extraordinary new sensation of fullness. She saw a curse forming on his lips and leaned down to kiss the pulse point in his neck.

Cade sucked in a breath.

"There isn't much point in stopping now, is there?" she whispered.

For an answer, he drew her mouth to his in a kiss that began the race of thrills all over again. She sensed his anger just below the surface, but his hand slipped between their joined bodies, touching her in a way that sent coherent thoughts scattering to the wind.

Her breath quickened when he fondled one breast. He drew it into his mouth biting lightly on the nipple. She cried out as her body convulsed, overloaded by all the sensory input even as Cade drove to his own release.

She collapsed against his damp chest, physically and mentally spent. For a very long time, they lay there, while the world righted itself once more.

"Why didn't you tell me?" he asked quietly.

"I did. I said I'd never done this before."

His gray eyes were silvery, unreadable as he gazed at her.

"You knew I thought you meant this position."

"Yes. But I didn't want you to stop. And you would have."

"Damn right. You were a virgin."

The anger was back, tightly controlled, but there.

"I should have known."

"How? Was I that bad?"

He'd treated her with such incredible reverence she hated thinking she'd ruined his pleasure by not responding adequately.

He must have read something of her thoughts in her expression because his features softened and he touched her hair lightly.

"You are—" he swallowed "—a generous lover, Jayne. I knew your body was too tight, too perfect. A woman who had just given birth…you should have looked differently. Acted differently. I should have recognized all that from the start. Heather isn't yours."

"Obviously."

She wasn't sure what he meant, but his anger seemed to have dissipated. She turned her head into the palm of his hand and he caressed her face.

"You were telling the truth. Weren't you? About all of it?"

"Yes."

Cade closed his eyes. She didn't know if he believed her or not, but she rolled off him, lying beside him on the bed.

"Why me?"

The question shouldn't have surprised her.

"Why not you?"

"You're beautiful. You claim you're twenty-four. How come you were still a virgin?"

"Because it never felt right before."

Because I think I'm falling in love with you.

"No. Don't think it," he said abruptly, rolling over to face her and raising up on one hand.

"Think what?"

"What you're thinking."

She smiled. "Censuring my thoughts is going to be a tough job, don't you think?"

He didn't smile back.

"Happily-ever-after isn't on offer here, Jayne. If you've got some crazy notion that giving me your virginity means I'm going to declare my undying love for you, you're setting yourself up for disappointment."

His voice was kind, but the words lashed her all the same. She hid the hurt and smiled. "If you declared your undying love for me, I'd know you were the one who was lying. We've only known each other a few days."

"And you'll be gone come morning," he agreed.

That hurt more than she would have thought. They'd just shared the most intimate act of all and he was calmly talking about her leaving first thing in the morning?

"I tried marriage once," he continued relentlessly, sitting all the way up and reaching for his pants. "I won't make that mistake again."

"How would you feel about living in sin for a while?" she asked, trying for a playful tone.

He stopped in the act of zipping his jeans. "You won't be here a while. We're taking the baby into the sheriff first thing in the morning."

Anger, fear and something else—something she desperately wanted to believe was longing—stared at her from cloudy-gray eyes. He turned quickly and reached for his shirt.

But his expression had been enough. Her hurt dissolved as she thought about what she knew of Cade. He had this image of himself as some crusty old loner. Yet inside, there was a man who wanted more. A man who no longer believed in miracles.

She was going to have to teach him to trust.

"Of course we're taking her to the sheriff," Jayne agreed. "I never intended to become her full-time guardian. I just couldn't stand by and let them hurt her—or sell her."

Cade made a sound low in his chest that sounded remarkably like a growl.

"Besides, I need to let my family know that I'm all right."

"You have family?" He paused in the act of buttoning his shirt.

"Most people do."

"I don't."

And she remembered him saying something along those lines earlier.

"Well, I have three brothers, two parents and assorted cousins, aunts and uncles scattered across Texas. You're welcome to borrow a few, especially my brothers."

"Three brothers!"

"Don't worry, Cade, they won't be coming after you. Liam's a judge, Devlin's a cop and Rory's a horse trainer who works beside my dad."

"Oh, hell. What's your last name?" Cade demanded.

"Bateman, why?"

Cade swore. "H. L. Bateman's your father?"

"Heard of him, huh?" She knew her pride showed in her voice.

Cade stuffed his feet into his boots and tucked in his

shirttail. They both heard the sound of the front door opening.

"Cade?" Hap's voice carried clearly.

"Get some rest." Cade said without looking at her. He left the room without a backward glance, gently closing the door behind him.

She lay there for a long time, going over every moment in her head. Cade's reaction to the truth had been predictable. His lovemaking had not. It had far exceeded her expectations. But now she forced herself to examine her reasons for entering the relationship with Cade. Had she subconsciously wanted to tie Cade to her by giving him her virginity?

If that had been her motive, odds were it was going to backfire. He didn't trust her. She wasn't even certain he liked her.

But he wanted her.

He'd proved exactly how much in a most exciting way. Only they couldn't build a lasting relationship on sex. He'd already tried that and failed miserably. True, she wasn't Bonita, but Cade probably wouldn't see past that broken relationship.

So what did she want from Cade? Any number of men and boys had been willing to take her to bed over the years. Yet she'd never had any trouble resisting until now.

It was one thing to believe she was in love during the throes of passion. It should be another thing to examine her feelings in the aftermath.

But it wasn't.

Cade was a difficult person to know. Yet if she could get past his protective shell, there was a wonderful, caring man inside. Look how he handled Heather. He cared deeply about things and people. No matter what he thought, that hard shell had a crack a mile wide. Only if she forced her way inside, she'd have to be prepared for the consequences.

Cade would never tolerate a wife who was off someplace working as a private investigator. He needed a woman who was willing to become a rancher's wife—and a possible mother? A week ago that thought wouldn't have sent longing racing through her. Did that mean she was ready to give up her new career?

"Ha! Think about all those mind-numbing hours sitting on stakeouts. Think about all those sad people wanting dirt on their boyfriends. There isn't all that much to give up." Even the exciting parts hadn't been all that great, she decided ruefully, touching the bandage over her shoulder.

But having Cade's baby…

JAYNE DIDN'T REMEMBER falling asleep, but when she woke it was dark. A small night-light cast a soft glow around the room. A sandwich, an apple and a brownie sat on the nightstand, thoughtfully wrapped. Alongside was a cup that must once have held ice, but now contained melted water. Beside it was a small bottle of apple juice.

And Heather wasn't in the room.

For a moment she panicked, then she realized Cade must have the baby. The silence in the house was complete, but she knew in her heart the sheriff had never arrived or Cade would have woken her. Besides, the baby-nappers would never go anywhere near the sheriff's office. She didn't have to worry about that problem until morning.

She was ravenously hungry, but she needed to go to

the bathroom. That meant getting dressed. Who knew who might be out in the hall?

Jayne reached for the jeans and the shirt she'd worn earlier to find Cade had taken them. In their place he'd left her own clothing cleaned and folded. Her blouse was too sheer, too stained, and too damaged to wear without a bra. He must have recognized that fact because he'd also left her a new T-shirt and a short-sleeved denim shirt.

As she dressed, her gaze drifted toward the window. A flash of movement near the barn riveted her attention. Two figures stood in the deep shadows talking.

Cade?

She couldn't tell.

As she watched, one person melted back inside the barn. The other started toward the house. Jayne strained to see. The person heading toward the house was thin to the point of slender, with long dark hair pulled back in a ponytail. For an instant, the moon obliged her wish, lighting the scene enough for Jayne to glimpse the stranger's face. Then the clouds took away the light and the person moved out of range.

Heart pounding, she ran to the box on the floor, nearly falling over it in her hurry. She didn't want to turn on any lights and alert the person to her presence.

Mostly by feel, she dug through the items until she came to the picture that had fallen from Bonita's boot. She hurried out into the hall and into the bathroom where she turned on the light and stared at the two faces closely.

Either Bonita had come back from the dead or Luís was here on the Circle M.

Jayne ran to Cade's door and opened it without knocking. "Cade?"

He lifted his head immediately. "Jayne? What's wrong?"

He threw off the sheet revealing his bare chest, though he wore jeans and socks. His shirt lay on the nightstand. Jayne realized he could be fully dressed in a heartbeat.

"What's wrong?" he repeated.

"Two people were out by the barn. I saw one of them. You were right. Your brother-in-law is here."

Cade swung his legs off the bed, shoving his feet inside his boots with no wasted motion. "You saw him?"

"Yes, but I didn't see who he was talking with."

Heather was sleeping peacefully in the center of Cade's double bed.

"Stay with the baby." He grabbed his shirt. Underneath was a handgun.

"Wait! What are you going to do?"

"Wait here."

"But—"

He was gone, moving silently and swiftly before she could finish her protest. She really was going to have to break him of that irritating habit he had of not listening to people.

Cade hadn't bothered to shut the bedroom door. Still, it was only because she was straining so hard to hear that she recognized the squeak of the door hinges across the hall. She leaped out of bed and ran to the doorway. Zed stood in the hall, one hand on the guest room door. Was he leaving, or coming in? He was fully dressed down to the rifle.

"You startled me," he said. "I heard someone moving around."

"Do you always go to bed fully dressed?"

"I do when I'm expecting trouble. What about you?"

Other than footwear she realized she, too, was fully dressed.

"I saw two men over by the barn. Cade went to check it out."

Zed swore. "I'd better give him a hand."

"No! It's too dark outside. He won't be able to tell friend from foe. Someone might get hurt."

"I don't reckon it's my hide you're worryin' about now, is it? It's okay, Jayne. You probably saw Hap and Rio changing places. They were gonna take the late shifts keepin' an eye on things. I took the first watch."

"Well you didn't do a very good job. Luís was heading toward the house."

Zed stilled. "You saw him?"

"Yes."

"You might have been dreaming."

"I wasn't."

He started for the living room.

"Zed, get back here! Cade might shoot you by mistake."

"I might just shoot you on purpose, too," Cade said, suddenly filling the other end of the hall. "Going somewhere?"

"I was goin' out there to keep you from doin' somethin' stupid."

"And what might that be?"

"Jayne says she saw Luís outside."

"If she did, he's gone now. You got dressed awful fast, Zed."

"I was sleepin' in my clothes, same as you, I expect. You didn't find anyone?"

"No one to find," Hap said at Cade's back. "I don't know what she saw, but I just walked through the barn.

There was no one there. Nor any sign someone had been there.''

"I saw Luís D'Angelo," Jayne insisted stubbornly.

Hap shoved his hat back on his head. "You know him?"

"No, but I've seen his picture."

"It's a very dark night, ma'am."

"The moon came out. I saw his features clearly."

"Well, he's gone now," Cade interrupted.

Jayne couldn't tell if he believed her or not. "What about the person I saw him talking to? Where's Rio?"

"In the bunkhouse. Asleep," Hap added.

"Are you sure?" she asked.

"There's one way to find out." Cade brushed past Hap who gave Jayne a sour look before turning and following. Zed frowned at her as well.

"I'm going with them. If Luís is nearby there should be signs of a horse or a vehicle. He sure didn't walk here."

Deflated by their reaction, Jayne used the bathroom, snatched up the plate of food, and returned to Cade's room to wait. His window was open with a view of the front of the house. She watched Zed head toward the far side of the house, away from the barn.

If only she'd gotten a better look at the second person. He'd been nothing more than a shadowy shape. It could have been any of the three men. Only one thing was probable. Cade had an enemy right here on this ranch. It was possible that the second person had been a stranger, but somehow, she didn't think so—and she said as much to Cade when he returned alone.

"Rio was in the bunkhouse," Cade said. "He says he was asleep."

"That's what Zed claims, too."

"And Hap never saw anyone."

"So he says. What are you going to do, Cade?"

"I'm going to try to get a couple of hours of sleep before dawn. You'd better do the same. We're leaving first thing in the morning."

Jayne tried not to show her hurt at this clear dismissal. She pulled off the denim shirt and reached for the hem of the T-shirt.

"What are you doing?" Cade asked.

"I was getting into bed. Should I keep the T-shirt on? Do you think any more will happen tonight?"

"You're not sleeping in here."

His words cut, but she didn't flinch. He was defining limits to protect himself. He didn't trust her or the emotions they'd shared tonight. It was up to her to show him that she wasn't Bonita and she knew her own mind.

"Well, if you think I'm spending the rest of the night alone, think again, Cade. I know what I saw even if the rest of you don't believe me."

"I believe you. But if you're looking for more sex—"

"Stop trying to provoke a fight. It's late and we're both too tired. With Zed across the hall and the baby in the bed with us, your virtue is safe." She offered him her most innocent smile. "At least for the rest of the night."

She got under the sheet on the far side of Cade's bed. He appeared flummoxed by her actions and her words. He stood in the dark indecisively, reminding her of that night in the line shack. Unlike that night, he didn't wait for her to point out how foolish he was acting. He pulled off his boots and lay down on top of the rumpled covers. The baby slept blissfully unaware between them.

"Are you okay?" he asked gruffly, breaking the silence that descended. "I didn't hurt you earlier?"

She smiled to herself in the dark. "No. You made it a nice experience. Right up until you turned hostile."

"Nice? What do you mean, hostile?"

"Don't worry about it. As you said, in the morning I'll be gone and you won't have to think about me again."

She could practically hear him mulling that over. She decided it was time to give him something more important to worry about. "Cade?"

"Hmm?"

"Is it possible that Bonita isn't dead?"

He jolted to a sitting position. "What?"

"Because I've been thinking about the person I saw—slender, with long dark hair. In the picture, Bonita and her brother looked an awful lot alike."

Cade muttered something under his breath. The room fairly vibrated with new tension.

"The police said she died in that accident," he replied finally.

"But you don't know for sure. You let her brother claim the body. What if it wasn't her body? If she is still alive, then technically you two are still married. If anything happens to you, she inherits this entire ranch."

Silence stretched between them like a living presence.

"Get some sleep, Jayne," he said finally.

"Sure." Though after sleeping most of the evening away, that wasn't very likely. "And Cade? Thanks for making my first time so memorable."

She smiled as she heard him mutter, but she sobered quickly. What she'd told him was nothing less than the truth. She would ask her brother the cop to look into

Bonita's accident. If Bonita *was* dead, then Cade was up for grabs. And she planned to be the one doing all the grabbing. She'd use a crowbar if she had to, but she was going to peel away that outer shell he kept around his heart and his emotions. There was a good man inside. One who needed to learn how to laugh and love.

She was the perfect woman to teach him how.

Chapter Ten

In the morning, Cade knew he had a problem. The sane, sensible thing was to drive Jayne and Heather into town, drop them at the sheriff's office and forget about them.

He wasn't sure exactly when he'd gone mad, but he wanted Jayne to stay.

At least for a while.

Until he got her out of his system?

It wasn't just sex, though that was confusing the issue. Making love with Jayne had been something he would never forget in a million years. She had taken his orderly life and twisted it until he was starting to look at his existence from a whole new perspective. That alone was unsettling, but one question continued to haunt him.

Why?

Why would a woman who looked like Jayne hang on to her virginity for twenty-four years only to give it to a stranger? He was afraid she had confused gratitude with some stupid romantic notion of falling in love. And it really scared him because the idea of Jayne being in love with him was altogether too pleasing.

Hadn't he learned anything from his time with Bonita?

Jayne wasn't Bonita. She was H. L. Bateman's daughter. The trainer was widely known in this part of Texas. Cade knew his work, though he'd never been able to afford a horse trained by the Bateman stables. But as his daughter, Jayne must have grown up on a ranch.

Sure. Only now she was a private investigator.

If she'd liked ranching she wouldn't be off chasing kidnappers for a living. The less time he spent with Jayne from now on, the better for all of them. Wanting her was bad enough, but if he let himself contemplate a future that included her... No. He wouldn't think about that.

After he finished feeding Heather her bottle, she gurgled happily up at him and he dabbed at the traces of spit and milk. What would Heather look like when she grew up? Would someone give her a good home? Love her the way she deserved? Or would she grow up like he had in a series of foster homes, finally rescued by a crotchety old man who hadn't known or cared how to share his emotions?

"I sure wish I knew someone would take good care of you, little one."

"She'll find a good home," Jayne said softly at his back.

Cade twisted and found her watching him from the hall. She was dressed as she had been last night. But it was the thin material of the T-shirt he'd left out for her that captivated his attention. The dark-blue material hugged the outline of her breasts, revealing the tempting profile of her nipples. Was she always going to have this power over him?

"Someone will be thrilled to have an adorable baby

like Heather,'' Jayne was saying. He forced his attention to her words and away from that bewitching body.

"You're right,'' he said getting to his feet. "I'll make you something to eat and then we'll head on into town.''

"I need to grab a shower first. Where is everyone?''

"Rio said his injured arm felt better so he and Hap just left to check on the herd. Zed went out to the barn to turn Lafferty out to pasture. He's going to ride into town with us to bring back Hap's truck after I pick up mine and have the tires fixed for the SUV out front.''

"So we're alone?''

"Except for the baby.''

"You're going to miss her, aren't you? Me, too,'' she added before he could decide how to answer. "I've grown attached to that little girl.''

"But you'll soon be busy with your next big case.'' He thought he did a credible job keeping the bitterness out of his voice. Jayne smiled. It was a secretive, womanly smile that made him nervous.

"I don't think so, Cade. The glamour and excitement of being an investigator wore off the minute those two hoods pulled out guns and started shooting at me.''

He stilled the momentary hope that crowded his thoughts. "You'll change your mind once your shoulder heals and you get back home.''

"No. I don't think I will.'' Her gaze was clear as she stared at him. "I suspect my mind is going to be very occupied thinking about a stubborn cowboy who's afraid to take a chance.''

Cade's entire body clenched. There was no mistaking that challenge.

"What do you want from me, Jayne?''

"Are you going to pretend nothing is happening between us?"

"No. I told you I wanted you. I still do. Is that what you want to hear?" He knew his words hurt her. They hurt him almost as badly, but if she was looking for a declaration of undying love...

"Okay. If that's all you have to offer I'll take it," she replied sounding sadly resigned.

His gut tightened another notch. He couldn't pretend to misunderstand her words and they tore at him.

"Go get your shower."

"You could scrub my back."

His mind painted the picture while his body prepared for action.

"Stop it, Jayne. We don't have time for that this morning."

She tipped her head, her hair rippling in a fascinating wave over one breast.

"We could make time. If you want to."

Oh, he wanted to all right. He wanted to take a long time for an extensive, slow loving. Jayne was highly sensual, an eager, untutored lover. Her body was responsive to the slightest touch. Loving her heightened all the senses.

And she was H. L. Bateman's daughter. Way out of his league.

"No."

The expectant light faded from her eyes.

"You know, Cade, being a loner isn't a disease. It's a choice."

He stared after her, mesmerized by the sway of her hips as she disappeared back down the hall. Heather's tiny hand wrapped around his finger, much the way she'd wrapped herself around his heart. And Jayne's words echoed painfully in his mind.

CADE AND ZED HAD JUST finished emptying the back of the truck and putting the slashed tires inside when Jayne joined them holding Heather. Seeing her standing there in the sunlight stole his breath away.

"'Mornin'," Zed said, smiling at her.

Cade wanted to hit him.

His gut gave a lurch. She'd taken off her slacks and was wearing a long, brightly colored full skirt and a white T-shirt. No doubt the skirt had belonged to Bonita, and Jayne must have taken another shirt from his dresser drawer. He told himself there was nothing intimate about that. Not after what they'd shared. She'd needed a shirt and she'd borrowed one. But his brain seemed fascinated by the image of her in his room, going through his things.

Over the T-shirt she had draped the shawl that she'd used as a makeshift sling the other day. Her hair sparkled like white gold, shiny in the morning sunlight. Strands fell over the soft swell of her chest. She looked young and beautiful enough to create a sense of panic in his orderly thoughts.

And Zed was still smiling at her.

"Good morning, Zed," she replied. "Are we set to go?"

Zed leaned back against the truck bed, his gaze going from one to the other. Cade knew he sensed something in the charged atmosphere that seemed to surround Jayne and him like a glass bubble.

"I'll need to change your bandage first," Cade said tersely, trying to break the spell.

"That won't be necessary. It's fine. I covered it with

some plastic wrap and didn't wash my hair. The bandage isn't even damp. I'm set to go whenever you are.''

Had she done that so he wouldn't have an excuse to touch her again? The thought was raw.

Zed came off the truck. ''Here, Jayne, you want me to hold Heather for you while Cade puts her car seat in place?''

''Thank you, Zed.''

Cade set his jaw. His temper sizzled. He couldn't stand watching her with Zed, so he strode into the house, brushing past her without a word. He lifted the car seat and the diaper bag, then turned around to find her silently watching him.

''I wasn't flirting with Zed,'' she said quietly.

''I didn't say you were.''

He hadn't even thought it, not really. It just made him…edgy…to think about her with another man. Especially Zed.

''Your actions did.''

''I came in to get the stuff so we can get going, all right?''

For a long moment she just stood there. A shadow crossed her features. He wanted to call back his abrupt words, but she gave a sad nod and turned back to the door.

He should say something. They shouldn't part like this.

Cade swore mentally. He'd never been any good with words or emotions. He couldn't think of anything to say that wouldn't raise a false hope in her. He wanted to beg her to stay, but he had no right. She was young. Too young for him, anyhow. And he wasn't ever getting married again. Especially not to someone as beautiful as Jayne—even if she had grown up on a ranch.

She'd forget all about him soon enough. She'd be back home this afternoon. Back where she belonged.

And he'd be alone again.

The way he liked it, he told himself firmly. Cade carried the stuff outside and tried not to look at her. She stood talking softly to Zed.

Zed appeared totally comfortable holding Heather. That only set Cade's back teeth on edge again. As Cade fit the car seat in place, he couldn't stop the stab of possessiveness that lanced him. This was nuts. Heather wasn't his any more than Jayne was. If Jayne wanted to flirt with Zed it was none of his business. Now that she wasn't a virgin anymore she'd probably find dozens of lovers lining up outside her door. The image infuriated him.

"Want me to drive?" Zed offered.

"No," he snapped. "I'll drive."

Zed raised his eyebrows in surprise. "Sure, Cade. Whatever you want. I'll climb in back with Jayne. Heather sure is a cutie."

"Isn't she?" Jayne agreed. "She's such a sweet-tempered baby. I'm not sure how I'm going to give her up."

Frustrated, Cade waited for the two of them to get in back. If he'd let Zed drive, he could have ridden in back with Jayne. But he remembered all too well the ride here with her thigh pressed against his. Enduring that again this morning would be pure hell.

He was turning into a nutcase. There was nothing in the back seat crowding them together. They sat a respectable distance apart. Yet he wished he'd let Zed drive. The ride into town had never taken so long.

Zed chatted away, talking about the rodeo circuit and towns they'd been in. Jayne listened and even asked a few questions. Cade tried and failed to think of something to contribute besides monosyllable answers whenever one of them directed a question or a comment his way. More than once, he caught Zed's amused glance in the rearview mirror. He wanted to stop and wipe that smug look right off the other man's face. He failed to see anything amusing about any of this.

"I'll drop you at Sully's to pick up my truck," he said abruptly. "Then I'll take Jayne to the sheriff's office. Check the radio in the truck before you do anything else. If it's been tampered with, take it straight over to Rafferty and see if he can have a look at it. If not, go back to the ranch and keep an eye on things until I get there."

"Sure, Cade. You don't want help with the tires?"

"Not until I have to put them back on the truck. You can help me then."

"Yippee."

Jayne smiled at Zed. Cade gnashed his teeth.

"Sounds like a busy day all around."

Zed met his gaze in the mirror. "Yeah. Busy." He looked away. "Imagine your family will be glad to have you back," Zed told Jayne.

"Especially my brothers. They live to tease me."

"Where do you—" He broke off to stare out the window. "Whoa, now. That's mighty interestin'," Zed drawled. "Wonder what brings Zach Logan clear out this way."

"Who's Zach Logan?" Jayne asked.

Cade followed their glance to the front of the squat brick building that housed the sheriff's office. A tall thin, middle-aged man with a mustache was striding toward a sedan parked in front. His dark, neatly pressed suit and stark white shirt were as out of place in this setting as his car.

"Zach Logan used to be the chief of detectives for the Dallas Police Department," Zed told them. "Might still be for all I know. Darwin Crossing is way the heck out of his jurisdiction."

"You know, I think I've heard one of my brothers mention him," Jayne said.

"He's made the news more than once. I think he's even had his picture in the paper with Governor Kincaid." Zed pointed straight ahead. "That your missin' truck, Cade?"

"Yeah."

Jayne's attention swung to the pickup truck. From her expression, Cade knew she was remembering just as he was. It seemed a lifetime ago that she'd crawled into the back of his truck to hide. The pickup sat in the far corner of the empty parking lot. As they pulled up, Cade saw that the heavy feed bags were still inside.

Cade pulled up and fished out the spare set of keys. "Here, Zed. I'll see you back at the ranch."

"Sure. Jayne, you take care of yourself, okay?"

"I will. Thanks, Zed."

He touched her hair lightly before he stepped out of the truck. Cade barely contained an urge to hit him. As if sensing this, Zed paused. He looked at Cade and shook his head.

"Dumber than mud," he said cryptically. "Bye, Jayne."

Cade gritted his teeth. As soon as Zed was clear he pulled out quickly raising a cloud of dust and gravel.

"What did that mean?" Jayne asked.

"Just Zed being cute."

"Gee, I'm surprised he's your type."

"Wh— Oh. You have a warped sense of humor."

"So my brothers tell me."

Coming up on the sheriff's office from this angle, the first thing he saw was the side parking lot—and a familiar silver car. Adrenaline charged his system.

"Don't stop!" Jayne cried, leaning over the seat. Obviously, she'd spotted the car, too. "Keep going!"

"No. I won't let him hurt you, but it's time we put an end to this, Jayne. We need to go inside and—"

The gun appeared over the seat from nowhere. His gun. The one he'd given her to protect herself with the other day. Now Jayne pointed it at his head.

"Keep driving, Cade. I mean it."

For a second, he stared at her, unable to believe his eyes.

"Go! Now!"

He could reach out and grab the barrel. He was pretty sure she wouldn't shoot. But her fear was so great the gun could go off accidentally. He pressed on the gas and continued past the sheriff's office while he debated the best way to calm her fears.

"We both know you aren't going to pull that trigger," he said mildly, tamping down the surge of emotions that threatened his control.

"I am not taking Heather in there so that man can tell some gullible hick sheriff his lies and walk off with this baby. Not after everything I went through to save her."

"In the first place, what makes you think Sheriff Beaufort is a hick, let alone gullible? And in the second place—"

"You didn't believe me. You *still* don't believe me. Not entirely, do you?"

"Jayne—"

"You don't, do you? Well I don't care. Put on some speed. What's the next nearest town? Never mind. You can take me home."

"All the way to Bitterwater? That's over thirty miles!"

"Then you'd better get going."

Time to control this situation.

"I don't think so."

He steered the car to the shoulder and rolled to a stop.

"What are you doing? Keep going!"

"No."

Reaching out, he removed the gun from her hand. Her eyes widened in alarm. A glance at the gun showed the safety was on. He wasn't surprised. He'd known she had no intention of hurting him. What did surprise him was that she'd tried such a stunt in the first place.

"We're going back to talk to Beaufort."

"For once, just once, will you please listen to me?"

Her blue eyes were wide with entreaty.

"These men are dangerous, Cade. My brother said some of these babies may be kidnapped. They coerce or threaten young girls into giving up their infants. And they'll kill anyone who gets in their way. I've got a bullet wound in my shoulder to prove how serious they are. If I walk into that police office it could set off a bloodbath."

"Take it easy, Jayne. You're exaggerating."

"Am I? The men who came out to your ranch had phony IDs. Who knows what sort of ID this man has, or what story he may have told your sheriff. If the sheriff decides to listen to me, what do you think this man is going to do, calmly sit there and wait to be arrested? We have to go somewhere else. Someplace where I can call my brother. Trust me, Cade!"

Her fear was real. So was the bullet wound. And the man in the silver car had originally claimed to be her husband. Plus, she'd been right about the two men yesterday. They hadn't sent Beaufort out to the house.

Before he could tell her that he did trust her, he saw Zed pulling up behind him. The cowboy stepped from the truck and started toward the SUV. Jayne was out of the vehicle, running back to Zed.

She'd run to Zed.

"Hey there, easy now," Zed was saying as she repeated her story for the other man.

"Go back to the ranch," Cade ordered sharply, striding up to them.

"Hold up, Cade. I think you should listen to the lady."

"This isn't your problem."

Zed looked from one to the other. "Damn. You have to be the dumbest man on the planet."

"Get out of here, Zed."

"If you're too stupid to listen—"

"Stop it!" Jayne demanded. "Both of you, stop it! We don't have time for male posturing. I have to get away from here!"

"Get the baby," Zed said.

For a moment, blind rage threatened to take control of Cade's emotions. The last time that had happened was when Cade found his wife in Zed's arms. He'd nearly shoved the other cowboy through a wall then. This was worse somehow. He wanted to kill his former friend.

Cade forced back the fury riding his chest. "Stay where you are, Jayne. You're fired, Zed."

"Fair enough," Zed agreed "but Jayne is coming with me."

"Over my dead body."

"What is wrong with the two of you?" Jayne whispered.

"Cade has a problem with his listening skills."

Jayne had told him the same thing.

"Get back in that truck right now, Zed or I'll do worse than try to put you through a wall."

"Damn." Zed took a step forward. "Dumber than mud."

Cade saw the punch coming. He blocked Zed's swing with his arm but his fingers went numb as the blow struck a nerve. Before he could recover, Zed landed another strike against his jaw that sent him reeling. Zed followed with a body blow. Air whistled from Cade's lungs even as his own fist bounced off the other man's shoulder. He started to lunge forward when a familiar silver car pulled alongside them on the road. A tall, muscular man jumped from the car.

Cade recognized him instantly.

"Break it up," the newcomer ordered. He started reaching inside his suit pocket.

Cade leaped forward even as Zed yelled a warning. "He's got a gun!"

Cade smashed his fist into the bigger man's stomach. Zed circled around behind, pinning the man's arms so he couldn't move.

"I'm a cop!" The man wheezed.

"That's what they all say," Zed told him.

"Hold him while I get his wallet," Cade ordered.

"And his gun," Zed agreed.

Cade removed the semiautomatic weapon from the belt clip. There was a wallet and an identification folder. He opened the folder and frowned.

"What is it?"

Cade held up the folder so Zed could read the badge as well. Zed swore. Cade opened the wallet. "The driver's license matches the identification card."

· "Aw, hell. Better release him."

Zed stepped back quickly. The man leaned forward, planting his hands on his well-muscled thighs, breathing heavily.

"Dallas Police Department?" Cade asked.

Zed's expression turned rueful. "I got a bad feeling it isn't fake."

"Of course it's not fake," the man identified as Dylan Garrett said.

"Two men showed up at my ranch claiming to be FBI agents yesterday," Cade told him. "They had badges, too, only we're pretty sure they weren't who they said they were."

Dylan straightened up. "Burly guys in bad-fitting suits with red ties?"

Cade and Zed exchanged glances.

"So they tracked her to you too. You are Cade McGovern, aren't you?" Dylan asked rubbing his stomach. "You pack a pretty mean punch."

Cade stopped rubbing his sore jaw where Zed's fist had landed.

"I was on my way out to your place," the officer continued. "I'm looking for a woman."

"Your wife?" Cade asked sarcastically.

Garrett shrugged, not looking the least bit embarrassed. "She's a private investigator by the name of Jayne Bateman."

Cade heard the words, but he'd already stopped paying attention because he'd just realized Jayne was gone. He scanned the surrounding area. There was no sign of her anywhere nearby. She hadn't had time to get far, but he didn't have to look to know the baby was no longer in the car.

Zed followed his gaze. His expression said he'd come to the same conclusion. Jayne had run.

Cade faced Dylan Garrett. The policeman watched the two of them speculatively. Cade hesitated. Garrett was a big, good-looking man with a rugged muscular build. His light-brown hair was sun streaked and his hands were work roughened like a rancher's hands.

Cade's words were for Zed. "Officer Garrett may be a cop, but that doesn't make him a clean cop."

Zed arched his eyebrows, but nodded.

"What are you talking about?" Garrett demanded.

"Jayne believes you're part of the baby ring."

Garrett's hands fisted at his sides, then relaxed. "Of course she does. I understand that now. I thought she was part of the ring, too. This was all a large misunderstanding. Look, my boss had a tip about the exchange. Unfortunately, one of the thugs spotted me at the shopping center before I was close enough to intercept. He started shooting. Next thing I knew, this girl jumps in the car and takes off with the baby. I didn't know who she was so I gave chase."

His expression turned rueful. "She drove like a crazy person and I lost her. I was riding around trying to catch her again when I stopped for gas. That's when I saw you and asked if you'd seen her. I figured calling her my wife was easier than long explanations."

"How can we know if he's telling the truth?" Zed asked.

"I've got a cell phone in my truck," Garrett told him. "You can call Sheriff Beaufort or my boss, Zach Logan. Better yet, why not call one of Jayne's brothers? Judge Bateman can vouch for me."

Cade knew if he erred, he'd be putting Heather and Jayne at risk.

"Get the phone," he told Zed.

The tiny wail of a baby spun him around. Jayne stood up in the bed of the pickup truck. She had Zed's rifle in her hands and she was pointing it directly at Dylan Garrett. She had climbed in the pickup truck to hide again, he realized. And she might have gotten away with it if the baby hadn't given her away.

"Jayne, he said—"

"I heard what he said. You called him Officer Garrett. What's the first name?"

Cade scowled. "Dylan."

"That's what I thought. I have a different number for you to call, Zed. Call information and get the phone number for Finders Keepers. It's a detective agency outside of San Antonio."

Dylan Garrett relaxed. The corners of his mouth edged into a smile. "So you know my sister."

"Yes, I know Lily."

The smile became a grin. "That'll make this a whole lot easier. We run Finders Keepers together when I'm not coerced back to work for the Dallas Police Department. Glad to see you're all right, Ms. Bateman. After we found the car and all that blood, well, your brothers have been a bit upset. She has some pretty powerful brothers," he added as an aside.

Cade's relief was tempered by the knowledge that it was all over. There was little doubt Garrett was exactly who he claimed to be, and by the time the phone call was completed, there was no question in anyone's mind.

They adjourned to the sheriff's office where more telephone calls were made.

"Now that I see you up close, I can see the resemblance to your sister," Jayne told Garrett.

The man smiled easily revealing a single dimple. "We're twins."

"Lily said you were her younger brother."

"By eight minutes," he confirmed wryly. "And she doesn't let me forget it for a second."

"What's going to happen to Heather?" Cade interrupted.

Deputy Sheriff Stuckley glanced up from where he was making goo-goo noises at the baby. "Darn if she doesn't remind me of my granddaughter. Noah called social services. They've got someone on the way over right now."

Sheriff Noah Beaufort nodded in agreement.

"Foster home?" Cade asked grimly, remembering his own past all too clearly.

"Until we can determine her parentage," Dylan agreed. "They have foster homes that specialize in infant care. Don't worry, she'll be well cared for," he added more gently. "If there is no family, we'll put her up for adoption legally. She'll get a good home."

Something inside Cade tightened another notch.

"Well, tell whoever takes her to keep an eye on that umbilical cord. I've been putting rubbing alcohol on the area but it bled a little again this morning. I don't want it getting infected."

"You can tell them when they get here," Dylan said kindly.

Jayne walked over to where Cade rested on the edge of a desk. The expression in her eyes made the back of his throat tighten. She laid her hand in his. For just a moment he allowed himself to hold her slender fingers. He sensed her own grief at parting with the baby.

"I have to get going," he said gruffly.

"You'll wait until my brother gets here, won't you?"

Cade tore his gaze from the yearning he read in her crystal blue eyes. He dropped her hand and reached for his hat, shaking his head. "I have to get those tires fixed and the radio looked at."

"Phone company said they can't get to you until tomorrow at the earliest, but I'll be out to talk with you about these incidents later this afternoon," Sheriff Beaufort said. "I'll want to talk with Hap and your men."

"Fine. They should have the herd moved by now, assuming there're no more cut fences."

He was aware that Jayne watched him sadly. What did she expect of him? It was obvious she was waiting for him to say something more, but he'd told her he wasn't a forever sort.

He walked over and stroked the baby's cheek. So soft and beautiful. Like Jayne. He prayed they were right, that someone would adopt Heather right away and give her a loving, happy home.

"Have a good life, little one," he whispered.

She smiled that foolish baby smile of hers and the back of his eyes burned as they hadn't done since he was a boy. He pulled his hat down low and strode for the door. He couldn't bear to look at Jayne because he was afraid he'd make a total fool of himself if he did.

He had work to do. A ranch to run.

And he hadn't felt this empty since they came to tell him his parents were dead.

Chapter Eleven

In the three days since she'd been at her parents' ranch, there hadn't been a word from Cade. Jayne had been so certain he'd come to his senses. He loved her. She was sure of it. Together, they could adopt Heather and raise a few of their own children if only he'd stop being so stubborn. He was not too old for her and she was not Bonita.

So while her family fussed over her, alternating between chiding and comforting, her mind played out various scenarios for making Cade see what they could have together.

Watching him say goodbye to Heather had been almost harder than saying goodbye herself. She'd asked her mother to foster the infant, but social services placed Heather with someone who specialized in infant care, as Dylan Garrett had said they would do.

As a young single woman, it was no use trying to adopt the baby herself when so many couples desperately yearned to give an infant a good, two-parent home. But she missed Heather's soft cries and wide baby smiles.

And she missed Cade.

She leaned against the fence post and watched her brother Rory working with a new, high-spirited mare.

"He's got a real knack," her father said.

Jayne offered a weak smile. "It's genetic, Dad."

"Possibly," he said seriously. "You have the gift as well."

Her mouth dropped in surprise.

"Your mother says you have to follow your own course," her father said absently, "but I always hoped one day you'd join Rory and me."

"I didn't know that."

Her father shrugged. "Your mother said if I told you, you'd think it was to keep you from trying your hand at this detective business."

Ruefully she accepted his words. "Mom's probably right. I might have thought exactly that."

"You're mother's generally right, girl. You need to keep that in mind. We're both a little worried about you, Jayne."

"Why? The doctor says my shoulder is healing fine. Oh. You mean me going back to work as a detective?"

"That too, but...you seem different. Distracted. Is there something you want to talk about?"

Jayne wondered what he'd say if she told him she was in love with an ornery cowboy ten years her senior? "Nothing you'd probably want to discuss, Dad."

He twisted to regard her. "Why don't you try me?"

His wide blue eyes, so like her own, regarded her seriously. The need to talk to someone suddenly seemed overwhelming.

"I'm in love with a cowboy."

"I see." Her father turned away with a thoughtful expression and stared out over the fence. Jayne was pretty sure he wasn't really watching his son work the fractious horse.

"This cowboy doesn't feel the same way?" he asked after a few minutes.

Jayne turned her attention to her brother as well.

"I think he does, but he was married before. It didn't work out. If he'd just open his eyes, he'd see that I'm nothing like her!"

"Divorced?"

"No. She ran off with one of his hands and died in a car accident."

At least everyone believed that. She never had gotten around to asking her brother the cop to run a check on Bonita's death.

"Do you see your brother Rory out there?"

Jayne jerked her thoughts from that direction to watch as Rory stroked the mare's neck, speaking low to her.

"Sort of hard to miss him, Dad."

Her father ignored the jibe.

"Courting a person's a lot like courting a horse. The critter's usually skittish and half wild. You don't charge up to him and throw a saddle over his back. Especially not if he's been abused, Jayne. And there's some horses that it's best not to put a saddle on again."

She stared emptily at the corral, her father's words creating an ache in the back of her throat.

"You can break any horse to saddle, sweetheart. But if you break his spirit, he isn't worth much in the long run."

She struggled against the burning sensation and turned to her father. He pulled her into his arms and held her as he hadn't done since she was a child.

"Then what am I going to do?"

Her father smiled down at her. "Show me what sort of trainer you are."

"Jayne!"

She gave her father a thankful squeeze and wiped away her tears with the back of her hand as her mother approached holding the telephone receiver.

"Phone call, Jayne. It's some cowboy."

Her gaze met her father's as she suddenly felt brimming with elation.

"Some horses are worth the work. Thanks, Dad. I'll remember what you said."

She took the instrument from her mother with a quick thank you and set off toward the house for some privacy.

"Now what was that all about?" she heard her mother ask.

"Our little girl just grew up."

HE'D CALLED.

Finally.

"Hello?"

"Jayne?"

Her hopes and dreams dashed themselves against reality as she recognized the voice. "Zed?"

"Yeah. Look, sorry to call you like this, but I don't know anyone else close by to call."

"What is it? Is it Cade? Is something wrong?"

"You could say that. We're in jail."

"In jail!" Her mind reeled with possibilities. "What happened?"

"Uh, could the explanations wait? Deputy Stuckley's getting a might impatient here. Look, Jayne, is there any chance you could come and, uh, bail us out?"

"You're in Darwin Crossing?"

"'Fraid so."

Cade was in jail.

"It will take me almost an hour to get there."

"We aren't goin' anywhere."

"Okay, I'm on my way."

"Jayne?" he interrupted before she disconnected. "Don't expect too much, okay? I've never ridden a meaner bull in my life."

"Are you talking about Cade?"

Zed grunted an affirmative. "He won't be happy to see you. Well, he probably will be, but he won't want to admit it."

You don't charge up to them and throw a saddle over their back.

Her father's word echoed in her head.

"Okay, Zed. I understand. I'll be there in an hour."

"Take your time, darlin'. It's my turn to judge the cockroach races anyhow."

She managed a smile that quickly faded as she disconnected and walked inside the house. Cade and Zed were in jail. What was going on?

An hour and ten minutes later she walked into the sheriff's office in Darwin Crossing. She'd taken the time to change clothing, comb her hair and run a tube of lipstick over her lips. She knew she looked cool and in control no matter what her insides felt like. The blue shirtwaist dress with matching high heels complemented her eyes. And because she'd be seeing Cade, she unbuttoned an extra button in front. Her heart raced in anticipation.

"Afternoon, Miz Bateman."

"Deputy. I came to post bail for Cade and Zed."

"Little late for Cade. I released him half an hour ago. Once he dried out and got over whatever was eating at him, he was willing to pay the fine and cover the damages over at Sully's.''

Her excitement shriveled away. Cade wasn't here.

"Dried out?''

Stuckley snorted good-naturedly. "That man was on quite a toot. Tore up Sully's place real good.''

"He was drunk?''

Stuckley nodded. His wizened face seamed in the middle with a broad grin. "Drunk as a fool and meaner than a Brahma with his nu— Beggin' your pardon, ma'am. Let's just say it took three of us to pull him off Lithcolm.''

"Cade attacked Zed?''

"That's what everyone claimed. Neither of them will say a word about what started things. Sully agreed to drop the charges providing someone paid for the damage. Cade agreed.''

"But you're still holding Zed?''

"Well, ma'am, it's this way. Cade was some kind of angry at Lithcolm and I'm not real sure he's calmed down yet. As of now Lithcolm doesn't have a job or means of support, no money and no place to go. That makes him—''

"My responsibility,'' she said decisively. "He works for me now.''

The deputy couldn't get those shaggy brows any higher on his forehead. He gave a low, tuneless whistle. "Does he now?''

"May I see him?''

"Lithcolm? Sure. He's the only one back there right now. Follow me.'' He opened a door and led her down a hall where he unlocked another door. "Lithcolm? You got company.''

Zed stood up inside the tiny prison cell. His good

looks had been supplanted by a black eye, a split lip, a bruised jaw and split and bruised knuckles. She was startled by the sight despite Stuckley's warning.

Zed eyed her in masculine approval, but he didn't ogle or leer. Still, she wished she hadn't left that extra button undone.

"Who won?" she managed to ask.

Zed grinned. Some of the tension went out of his shoulders. "He did." And he pointed at the deputy.

"That's my job. I'll leave you two to talk. You just holler when you're ready to leave, Miz Bateman."

"What happened, Zed? Is Cade okay?"

"That's a matter of opinion. He's too darn stubborn to see what's as plain as day to the rest of us."

"Enlighten me. What was the fight about?"

"Uh…" He looked down at his scuffed boots.

"Zed?"

He frowned uncomfortably. "I told him if he wasn't coming after you, I…uh, was."

"What?"

Zed knuckled his bruised chin. "Guess I should have waited until he sobered up but I'd never seen him drunk before. One, two beers, that's always been his limit. No hard stuff. Now I know why. He went from morose to furious in three seconds flat. It took four men to bring him down."

Stunned, she tried to assimilate his words. "Was he hurt?"

Zed gave a bark of laughter, shaking his head ruefully. "I don't think I laid a finger on him. And I'm just fine, thank you for asking."

She felt the blush work its way up her cheeks. "I didn't mean—"

"It's okay. Any chance you could post my bail so I

could get out of here? I think it's time I keep ridin' north. Looks like I overstayed my welcome.''

"I'll do you one better. My dad has a ranch in Bitterwater. How would you like a job?''

Zed stared at her. "I think I'd rather continue livin' if you don't mind.''

"You'd be working for my father, not me.''

"I'm not sure Cade would differentiate.''

"He will after I talk to him. And if you'd rather not stay there, Dad knows all the local people. I'm sure we could find you some work on another spread.''

Zed stared at her, his dark gaze unreadable. "Funny. I was under the impression you didn't like me.''

Jayne thought about how to answer that charge and decided on the truth.

"I don't like any man who uses looks and charm to get what he wants. And I'm not sure I trust you. Not entirely. But you did save my life so I owe you. And I figure if I get you a job over near Bitterwater, then you can't be over here causing havoc on Cade's ranch.''

Her words tightened his features, but he nodded. "You probably won't believe me, but I had nothin' to do with what's happenin' at Cade's ranch.''

"What about Bonita?''

"That tramp?'' His eyes grew angry and his fists gripped the bars. "I tried to warn Cade about her right from the start, but he wouldn't listen. I still think she slipped him somethin' that night they got married. That whole thing never did ring true. Like I said, Cade's not a drinker, but he got so lit that night he claimed he didn't remember anything.''

"Obviously, he can't hold his liquor.''

Zed shook his head. "I told you, he doesn't drink. He always claimed it was a family curse or somethin'.

His daddy got drunk and shot his mother and her lover and then killed himself when Cade was a boy.''

''What?''

Zed nodded. ''Cade always swore he'd never let himself get that out of control. Claimed alcohol makes the men in his family mean.'' Zed rubbed his jaw. ''I guess he knew what he was talkin' about. Cade has a temper. I always knew that. But I never met a man with better control.''

She stared pointedly at his face. ''You call that control?''

The corners of his mouth lifted. ''You may be right. Anyhow, despite your low opinion of me, I would never fool with another man's wife.''

''But he caught you—''

Zed shook his head. ''Bonita set that up. She called me into the room. Said Cade was in the bathroom and needed help. Only there was no one in the bathroom and when I turned around she'd unbuttoned her blouse and threw herself into my arms. I was tryin' to push her away when Cade opened the door. He never gave me a chance to explain.''

''Why would she do that?''

''To make him jealous. And to pay me back for dumpin' her. She was a kid. A nasty, vicious, petty kid in a woman's body. She was dangerous as hell. I know he probably doesn't think so, but the best thing that ever happened to Cade was the day she walked out on him.''

''My, God, Zed. If you're telling the truth then—''

''Everything all right back here?'' Deputy Stuckley asked, opening the door.

Jayne spun around, her mind whirling with the implications of what Zed had told her combined with her own nagging suspicion. "Everything's fine. I'd like to arrange for Mr. Lithcolm's release."

"Are you sure about that, Miz Bateman?"

Not really. She might be making the worst mistake of her life.

"My father is going to give him a job."

The deputy raised his bushy eyebrows again. "He know that?"

She offered a weak smile and firmed up her voice. "Mr. Lithcolm helped save my life. The least I can do is help him in return."

"All right, Miz Bateman, but I don't think Cade's gonna be real pleased about this."

"With any luck, he won't even know."

The deputy scratched his jaw. "That would have to be some powerful kind of luck, ma'am, because I'm going to have to tell him when he asks."

Unfortunately, Jayne knew he was right. As they walked out into the afternoon sun, Zed stretched and took a deep breath. "You don't need to go to bat for me with your father. I'll settle for puttin' miles between me and Darwin Crossing."

"And how do you plan to do that? I don't see Lafferty anywhere nearby."

Zed closed his eyes as the realization hit him. "I rode into town with Cade."

"I thought he fired you."

"He did, but he changed his mind after you left. With Hap gone, he's so short-staffed he was even willin' to let me stay on."

"Look, we need to talk, Zed. I meant it about the job. I'm sure Dad will take you on. Unless...you didn't really mean what you told Cade about coming after me, did you?"

Zed grinned. A tiny prick of uneasiness replaced her calm.

"You're one beautiful woman, Jayne, but I'm not stupid, darlin'. And I don't trespass. You belong to Cade."

"I don't *belong* to anyone," she amended in annoyance.

"I stand corrected. The point I was tryin' to make to him was that he was actin' like a damn fool. I wanted to get under his skin and make him think. I had no idea my words would lead to all-out war."

"I'm not sure whether to thank you or tell you what an idiot you are. Where is Lafferty?"

"With my gear," he said ruefully. "At Cade's place."

"That's going to make things awkward."

"You do have a way with understatement. I'll need to go out there and—"

"Oh, no! I don't think so. Have you looked in a mirror? I'll pick up Lafferty after we get you settled at my father's place." She unlocked her car door and slipped behind the wheel. She wasn't sure she wanted to like Zed, but he was hard to dislike. And if he was telling the truth, Cade was angry over a misunderstanding that Bonita had deliberately created.

"Somethin' botherin' you?" Zed asked.

"Huh? Oh." She started to put the key in the ignition and stopped. "Zed, the other night when I saw someone out by the barn...were you really in the room across the hall in bed?"

His gaze held hers, unblinking. "Yeah. I really was. Until I heard Cade go past the door."

His expression said he didn't expect her to believe him, which was why she suddenly did. Jayne nodded thoughtfully. "I had a clear view of the person's face when they were coming toward the house. Did you ever meet Bonita's brother, Luís?"

"No. I didn't even know she had a brother. She didn't talk much about her background."

"I found a picture of the two of them in that box of her stuff Cade still has. Except for the age difference, they could almost be twins."

Zed frowned. "What are you thinking?"

"I know it sounds crazy, but I keep wondering, what if Bonita isn't really dead?"

His mouth fell open as he gaped at her.

"You can't be serious."

"Cade let her brother claim the body. What if it wasn't her? Or what if she didn't really die? What if she's terrorizing Cade for the sheer satisfaction of doing it? You said she was petty and vicious."

"For cryin' out loud, Jayne."

"If she is still alive, then they're still married. Guess what happens if Cade dies?"

Zed sat in stunned silence, broken only by the drumming of his fingers against the dashboard.

"The person I saw that night could have been a boy or a woman," Jayne persisted. "At least your reaction tells me one thing. I'm certain you weren't the one she was meeting over at the barn."

Zed stared at her shaking his head. "This is crazy. Only...you know, this would be just like her. She'd love toyin' with him like this. There must be some way to find out if you're theory is right."

"There is. My brother the judge, or my brother the cop, should be able to check the records for me. But if I'm right—"

"Cade's in danger."

"Yes."

"I think maybe we ought to go pay a visit to one of your brothers."

"Agreed."

She started the engine and pulled onto the street. As they passed the feed-and-grain store where it had all begun, a battered, rust-streaked pickup truck passed them and turned into the parking lot.

Zed swore. "Turn around!"

"What?"

"Turn around! Bonita or her double is inside that truck."

Jayne braked so sharply Zed was thrown against his seat belt. She spun the car in a wild U-turn.

"Where'd you learn to drive?"

"Police academy," she said tersely. As she tore into the lot, a person with long dark hair stepped from the truck and started for the building. Jayne pulled up behind the truck, blocking it in.

"Hey there, take it easy," Zed warned.

The dark-haired man with Bonita's features whipped around to stare at them. "What do you think you are doing?" he asked querulously.

Jayne was out of the car before Zed had unfastened his seat belt.

"Are you Luís D'Angelo?" she demanded in her most officious voice.

"Sí." His gaze flew from her to Zed and back again.

"We want a couple of words with you."

"Who are you?"

"We'll ask the questions," she told him. "You were out at the Circle M four nights ago."

The boy turned to run. Zed moved with deceptive speed. He grabbed the youth. Luís spun around and lashed out with his fist. Zed ducked. Then he did something with his feet that Jayne couldn't follow and brought the boy facedown in the dirt. In an instant he had the youth in a hold with his knee against the boy's back, pinning him to the ground.

"This arm'll snap like a twig if you don't hold still," Zed warned the boy.

Jayne swallowed her surprise. How had Cade managed to inflict so much damage if Zed could move like that?

"Call the sheriff, Jayne."

She reached inside her purse for her cell phone.

"Wait! Wait! What do you want to know?"

"Where's your sister?" Zed demanded.

"My sister? My sister's dead."

"Wrong answer, boy."

"She's dead, I tell you! You're breaking my arm."

"I'm gonna do a lot worse than that."

"But she's dead! She died in a car accident almost a year ago."

"I think he's telling the truth, Zed."

"Nah, he just needs the truth shaken out of him."

"No, I swear it on my mother's grave. Bonita is dead."

"Is that why you were out at the Circle M terrorizin' Cade?"

"Sí. I wanted him to pay."

Zed stood back and yanked him to his feet. His features were sullen, and angry, but if he was lying, she couldn't tell.

"You wanted to pay Cade back for what?"

"He beat my sister and he threw her out."

"He did not!" Jayne asserted.

"You're wrong, Luís," Zed said more softly. "Your

sister ran off with one of Cade's men when he refused to go back on the rodeo circuit.''

''You lie.''

''No,'' Jayne asserted. ''He's telling you the truth. Bonita didn't want to be a rancher's wife. When Cade wanted to settle down, she left him.''

''Señor Ramirez said they fought all the time. Mc-Govern beat her.''

''Who's Señor Ramirez?'' Jayne asked. It had to be Hap or Rio. Hap, who wanted to buy the Circle M. What did Rio want?

The sheriff's car pulled up before Luís responded to her question and they all turned their attention to the wizened deputy as he stepped from the vehicle.

''Now I thought you two were leavin' town. You like the jail so much you looking for another stay, Lithcolm? Let the boy go.''

''But Deputy, this is Luís D'Angelo. Bonita's brother,'' Jayne protested. ''He's the one behind all the incidents out at Cade's ranch. He cut the phone lines and slit the tires and—''

''No!'' Luís protested, struggling free from Zed's grasp. ''I never did those things!''

''All right now,'' Stuckley said, ''I think we should all go back to the office and—''

A dark sedan swung into the lot at a high rate of speed. The fender slammed into the deputy before he could turn around. His body was thrown over the hood to land like an empty sack on the hard ground, his back and neck twisted at an impossible angle. Zed shoved the boy to the pavement and ran toward Jayne, yelling at her to get down as the car swung to a stop and one of the baby-nappers aimed a gun out the window.

Jayne crouched down, her skirt swirling around her.

Her purse fell from her hand. The gun spat a stream of flame. She screamed as Zed fell to the ground, practically at her feet.

She started to go to him when someone grabbed her from behind, wrenching her bad shoulder as meaty hands closed over her in a viselike grip she couldn't break.

Jayne struggled as she'd been trained, but a blow to her head sent her senses reeling. She heard the gun discharge again. Luís fell back down beside his truck. As she was dragged, kicking and struggling toward the dark sedan, she saw Zed's bloody fingers closed over her cell phone.

"Where's the baby?" the thug demanded.

He shook her hard, bringing tears to her eyes as pain stabbed her bad shoulder. His breath smelled of coffee and stale cigarettes.

"I recognized that big guy with her," the other man said. "He was the guy with McGovern. The kid must be at the ranch."

"No!" she cried in alarm.

"Oh, yeah. I think that's exactly where you left the kid."

"You're wrong! We turned her over to the authorities."

"I don't think so, lady. Taking the baby was stupid, you know that. You want a kid that bad, you buy one like everyone else. You picked the wrong baby to steal."

"Lou, what if she's telling the truth?"

"She's not. Are you lady? 'Cause if you are, we'll have to put a bullet in this pretty little face of yours right here and now. We gotta have that baby back. The people we work with don't take excuses."

Her brain numbed with fear. "You killed Zed and Deputy Stuckley and Luís," she whispered, stalling for time. She prayed she was wrong about Zed and Luís, but she'd seen the deputy's body and she knew for certain he was dead.

"That's right sweetheart and if you don't tell the truth, you're next. Now where is the kid?"

"We turned her over to the authorities three days ago."

"Wrong answer, sweet lips."

For a moment she thought she would black out or vomit from the force of his slap. Apparently, he thought so, too, because he let her go and she sagged bonelessly against the back seat.

"Go to McGovern's place. We'll get the kid. Then we'll kill her and that smart-talking cowboy."

Jayne shrank against the back seat while her mind tried to see a way out. Hap and Rio and Cade's men would be totally defenseless against these two ruthless goons.

Jayne had never been so frightened or felt so helpless in her entire life. She'd never even gotten a chance to tell Cade she loved him.

Please, God, don't let anyone be at the ranch house when they got there.

Chapter Twelve

Cade sat in his favorite chair brooding. Sheriff Beaufort had promised to drive out in a few hours to talk with Hap. He'd warned Cade to stay close to the ranch until he got there. That was fine by Cade. He had plenty of work to do right there at the house.

But he didn't care.

He'd been a fool and he knew it. He'd gone into Sully's bar because Sully told him the kid might come back that night. He'd gotten drunk because…

Face the truth, no matter that it was painful. He'd gotten drunk because he wasn't paying attention. He'd been sitting there feeling sorry for himself and it was all Jayne's fault. Until she stormed into his life he'd been content. He'd had his life arranged exactly as he'd wanted it. His land, his work, his men…he hadn't needed any more than that. He hadn't looked at the house and seen the neglect. He hadn't missed a woman's companionship because he could have it whenever he wanted to.

A man could go to town, have a couple of drinks, a meal and some companionship with or without the sex and there were no strings attached. That had always been enough.

Until Jayne.

He couldn't get her out of his head. He'd spent two long days and nights fighting an urge to call just to hear her voice. It was nuts. But he wanted to tell her about his day—about the stupid cow that got stuck in the mud and took three of them to pull her out—about the stray cat that wandered into his barn and gave birth to a litter of kittens under the disgruntled eyes of his two neutered barn cats. He wanted to hear her thoughts on the recent calm around the ranch.

Hell. He just wanted to hear her voice. And Zed had made the mistake of walking into the bar when he was supposed to be catching a ride back to the ranch with Rio. Being Zed, he couldn't stop trying to needle Cade.

If he hadn't drunk that last drink, maybe it would have been okay. But probably not. Drunk or sober, when Zed said he was going after Jayne, something inside Cade snapped. The memory of Bonita and Zed was supplanted with an image of Jayne in Zed's arms, and Cade had lost his tenuous hold on any semblance of control.

Finding Zed and his wife together had hurt his pride. Finding Zed and Jayne together would destroy him.

Cade had overturned the table like in some dumb western movie. His fury knew no limits. He'd done his best to rip Zed's head off his shoulders. Of course, he was paying the price now. Still, his hand and jaw might hurt like the devil, but he took satisfaction from every blow. Jayne would be furious if she ever heard about it. He could almost hear her outrage.

Jayne with her sharp tongue and her soft mouth. Expressive eyes that saw too much—and not enough. He couldn't stop thinking about the way she had given herself to him. After waiting twenty-four years for the right man to come along she'd chosen him.

And he'd screwed the whole thing up.

Cade shifted in his chair, not wanting to pursue that thought, yet not able to leave it alone. What would it be like to come home every evening to a woman like Jayne and a little girl like Heather? Bonita had turned this ugly old house into a battleground.

Jayne would have turned it into a home.

Oh, they'd spar. They couldn't help it. They were both strong-willed people. But Jayne would stand toe-to-toe with him. She wouldn't use any of those feminine tricks Bonita had been so fond of. And the making up part…ah, now that would be worth every battle. Cade knew he'd be the one making most of the concessions, but that would be okay, because Jayne would pay him back late at night in the privacy of their room.

He stopped the thought cold, right there, but he couldn't stop thinking about Jayne. She'd done everything in her power to protect that baby. Imagine what she'd do to protect someone she loved.

And he'd let her walk away.

Cade swore and got to his feet. These kinds of thoughts hadn't left his head since he'd left the sheriff's office three days ago. He was going to spend the rest of his life sitting in this cheerless house if he didn't do something. The problem was, he didn't have a clue how to go about courting a woman.

But Zed knew.

Zed was one of the biggest flirts on the circuit. Everybody loved Zed. Everyone except Jayne. She'd seen right through his charm from the start. Still, he'd know the right words to use. All Cade had to do was swallow his pride and ask for some advice. But first he'd have to go into town and have the sheriff turn Zed loose. If nothing else, Cade owed Zed an apology and he knew it.

Knowing how to rope a steer and run a ranch used to be enough. Words were hard. He could manage the apology, but how did a man go about asking a woman to stay?

Maybe he could offer Jayne a proposition. She hadn't wanted to give up Heather any more than he had. If they got married, surely the judge would consider their adoption plea. Caring for her like they'd done must give them some edge with the court.

Only, what about Jayne's career? She'd claimed the glamour had worn off. That didn't mean she'd be willing to settle for being a rancher's wife, stuck out here in the middle of nowhere, alone most of the day.

Cade looked around at the dark, uninviting room. Like a thunderbolt it hit him. They didn't have to stay here. Hap was willing to buy the Circle M. With the money from the sale of his grandfather's ranch Cade could buy another place, maybe closer to her parents. Wherever she wanted to live was okay with him. As long as it was *with* him.

He slammed his fist into his palm and grimaced. His knuckles were still raw from the damage he'd done hitting on Zed. He suspected he was in danger of going mad, sitting here in the darkened room like this. There was only one solution. He had to talk with Jayne. She probably wouldn't want him—not even for the sake of Heather. But he needed to hear it from her.

He reached for his hat and the telephone rang. Cade eyed it like a rattler come to life. The house line seldom rang. It could only mean more trouble. He could ignore it and keep going, but it was probably Hap with news of the latest problem.

Cade cursed under his breath. It wasn't fair to constantly put the burden of ranch decisions on Hap's capable shoulders. His grandfather hadn't left the Circle M to Hap.

Scowling, Cade strode to the telephone.

"Yeah?" he barked into the receiver.

"They got her."

Zed's voice sounded weak and faraway. The line was filled with static, but he could hear Zed breathing hard in shallow gasps.

"What—?"

"...comin'...your way..." He ended on a pant as if the words had taken a lot from him.

Fear settled its mantle over him. Something was badly wrong.

"Who's coming? Zed? Talk to me. Where are you? Zed!"

For long seconds there was silence. He heard the phone smash against something. There was noise in the background. Voices. Zed was supposed to be in jail. Cade had left him there requesting that Sheriff Beaufort not release him until Cade had time to calm down.

A new voice suddenly filled his ear. Young, excited. A voice shrill with emotion.

"Hello?"

"Who is this?" Cade demanded.

"Luís D'Angelo. We need help. He is bleeding badly. I do not think he can survive. The deputy...I think he is dead. He's all crumpled together like a toy...."

What was Luís doing at the jail with Zed? Deputy Stuckley was dead?

"What the hell is going on?" Cade demanded.

"Two men in a dark car, they ran over the deputy. They shot this man and took the woman."

"What woman?"

But he knew. Cold certainty filled the hollows of his fear with dangerously dry ice.

"Jayne? They have Jayne?"

"Sí. They took the woman and drove away fast. We need an ambulance."

The boy's fear and shock helped Cade fight his own battle with panic. He forced his voice to a calm he was far from feeling as adrenaline coiled in his gut.

"Where are you?"

"Outside the general store."

Not inside the jail? Cade pushed aside the reason for Jayne to be with Zed outside the general store. Instead he concentrated on keeping the young voice calm on the other end of the staticky line. His fear was that he would lose the connection altogether.

"Is the deputy's car there?"

"Yes!"

No doubt someone had already called for help, but the boy needed something constructive to do.

"Go to the deputy's car. Find the microphone. Press the button and tell the dispatcher you need help. Tell them the deputy and others are hurt and you need a medivac unit. Give them your location. Do you understand?"

"Sí. I— What…? Señor, do not try to talk…. Sí. I understand. I will tell him."

Cade's fingers gripped the receiver hard enough to crush the plastic shell as he waited for the boy to come back on the line.

"The señor says to tell you they are heading for the

Circle M,'' the boy reported. ''He says they want the baby. They do not know the authorities have it. If they find out they will kill the woman.''

The world hovered on the brink of madness. The kidnappers had Jayne.

Cade forced himself to think. ''Tell Zed thanks and to hold on. Now go and call for help.''

''Sí.''

The cell phone clattered to the pavement. Luís had forgotten to turn it off. Cade disconnected and ran outside for the radio to call Hap.

Rio answered. ''Yeah, Cade?''

''Where's Hap?''

''Uh, I'm not sure. I think he was going after a stray. He should be back in a few minutes.''

Cade looked at the clock. It generally took about thirty minutes to get into town from here. If the kidnappers really pushed, they might be able to make it in fifteen. Little enough time to set a trap.

''Listen, Rio. Pass the word to the men. I've got two hired thugs on their way here to the ranch.''

''Those fake FBI guys?''

''Yes. They have Jayne and they want the baby.''

''But you don't have the baby.''

''I know that.'' He stilled his irritation and forced his voice to remain calm. As quickly as he could, he laid out the situation for the other man. ''They have already killed some people in town. Zed's been injured. If any of the men are willing, I could use some help, but I need it right now. When those guys get here and find out I don't have Heather anymore, they're going to kill Jayne. I figure I've got maybe fifteen minutes before they arrive.''

"Geez, Cade. It'll take us almost that long to get to you."

"I know."

And what good would four men really do, armed or not? His men weren't trained to go up against a pair of killers. Was he asking them to ride in here to their deaths? Rio surprised him before he could change his mind. With a forcefulness and a take-charge attitude normally foreign to the man, he responded.

"We're on our way, Cade. Stall 'em."

Cade closed his eyes in a mix of relief and gratitude. Then he spent several more of his precious minutes putting in a 911 call of his own. He repeated the information Zed had given him, added descriptions of the men and the car and explained the kidnappers were likely on their way to his isolated ranch with a hostage.

Feeling marginally better, he went back inside to hunt for the key to his grandfather's gun collection. He prayed the state police were close enough to have someone out here quickly. Otherwise it would be too late for him and for Jayne.

He unlocked the gun cabinet. Taking up a rifle, he reached for a box of shells. The box slipped from his hands. Bullets scattered across the thin carpeting. To heck with them. He was reaching for the second box when he heard the sound of a gun being cocked at his back.

Cade spun around. Hap stood behind him holding a .357.

"Geez, you gave me a start! How'd you get here so fast? Never mind. Give me a hand. We'll load as many of these—"

"Put the rifle down, Cade."

Something in his voice stilled Cade in the act of turning back to the cabinet. Death crawled up his spine as he remembered the sound of the hammer being cocked.

"What are you doing, Hap? The kidnappers are on their way out here with Jayne." His voice came out flat while his mind raced with wild possibilities.

"I know. I heard you on the radio talking to Rio."

Cade turned slowly. The .357 was pointed at his chest. At this distance Hap couldn't miss. The bullet would tear a good-size chunk out of his insides.

"What's this all about, Hap? Don't tell me you're working with the kidnappers?"

"Of course not. I'm simply taking advantage of the situation. This way is much better than setting fire to the house. I hated to have to take that step."

Cade felt his heart thudding painfully against his chest.

"Why would you consider a thing like that, Hap? Not that the ranch house doesn't need some major improvements," he added in weak bid for humor while he gauged the distance between them. Too far to lunge for the weapon. Hap was no fool. Cade would be dead before he ever reached the older man.

"I was willing to buy the ranch," Hap said sounding aggrieved. "You wouldn't sell. I'd hoped to make the sale more appealing by showing you all that could go wrong, but you're like your grandfather. Stubborn to the end."

Cade blinked, his mind trying hard to assimilate what Hap was saying—and what he wasn't saying.

"Are you saying you killed my grandfather? He died of influenza."

"He was ill, but we were arguing over his plans to give you the Circle M. He began to breathe too hard.

He clutched his chest and fell to the ground. I simply did nothing. In the end, he died.''

"You watched him die? You didn't give him his pills? Didn't try to help?''

Hap shrugged. He remained unmoved, his dour expression never changing.

Cade swore. "You were behind everything. You slit the girths, cut the fences—''

"No. I simply ordered it done.''

"Rio?''

Hap snorted in disgust, his first show of emotion. "Of course not. But your brother-in-law was quite willing to provide a little help in exchange for cash. Bonita laid the groundwork with her unhappiness. I embellished the story to suit my needs.''

"You lied to Luís,'' Cade said flatly.

"Of course I did. You should have stayed on the rodeo circuit with your pretty young wife, Cade. She liked to party.''

"You and Bonita?'' The idea shocked him all over again.

Hap shook his head, but the gun never wavered. "She was pretty, just as her name translates, but she wasn't interested in me that way. She just liked a sympathetic ear.''

"One that you helped fill with ideas?''

Hap's dark eyes gleamed smugly.

"Congratulations, Hap. I never saw this coming. You blindsided me completely. I know we have our differences in how things should be done, but I would never have suspected you. I trusted you.''

"A mistake,'' Hap said calmly.

"This is all about the ranch?'' Cade demanded, looking pointedly at the gun.

"What else? Your grandfather and I worked together from the day he bought the Circle M."

"I know. I considered you family."

Hap shrugged. "Again your mistake. You should have stayed on the circuit. Failing that, you should have sold me the ranch after Otis died. I thought when I encouraged Bonita to leave, you'd follow her. It was pathetically easy. So was convincing her that young Gordon had what it took to be your replacement on the circuit. You were supposed to go after them."

"And then what? Was Gordon going to shoot me?"

"I had hoped, given your temper, you might be the one to do the shooting."

"Sorry to disappoint you."

"It doesn't matter. You've given me another means entirely to get what I want—what I deserve. When I shoot you, the kidnappers will take the blame."

Cade shook his head. "You're forgetting about forensics. It'll never work. You have the gun."

"This gun can't be traced. One of the kidnappers will be found with it after I shoot them."

"You're fooling yourself, Hap. These guys are professionals. And what about Jayne? Are you going to murder her, too?"

"Of course."

Panic threatened to choke him. He pushed it back knowing he was Jayne's only hope.

"You're still forgetting about Rio and the others. Do you think they're going to stand by and let you kill all of us without saying anything. Or do you plan to murder three more innocents for a chance to buy the Circle M?"

"Rio and the others won't get here in time. You know that. They'll waste time searching for me. By the time they decide to leave without me, it will all be over. The timing will be close, but I think, not too close.''

''You're nuts. Forensic evidence will show that I was shot first. And I'm going to remind you again that these guys are professional killers. You won't be able to kill them.''

Hap shrugged. ''They won't be expecting an ambush. When they step from the car, I'll kill them. I am quite good with a rifle, you know.''

''Yeah.'' Cade knew. The picture Hap was drawing was vividly real.

''Who's to say when the kidnappers arrived, or what actually happened? You've made my job easy by getting involved with the woman. I could see you were thinking about bringing her back here, and that would never do. She might have stayed. Now put the rifle down.''

''There's some real irony here, Hap. I was just thinking of selling you the Circle M so I could buy a place closer to Jayne's family.''

His eyes narrowed. ''You should have sold me the ranch when I asked.''

''I don't suppose we can work out a deal now?'' Cade asked quickly.

This time the smile was genuine. ''No.''

Cade dove to the side. At the same time, Hap fired. The gun erupted with ear-shattering intensity. The acrid taste and smell filled the room. A burning pain seared the side of his rib cage. Something warm and wet began to mat his shirt.

The second shot went into the chair, inches from his head. There was nowhere to go. Hap started forward, bringing the gun into line. Cade tried to get up, all the while knowing he had no chance.

Fate intervened. Hap's leather boots skidded as he stepped on several of the loose bullets. The shot went wide because Hap had to fling out his arms to steady himself. Cade came up off the floor, swinging the rifle like a club. The stock caught Hap across the forehead. Blood welled from the deep cut, blinding the foreman. That didn't stop him from bringing the .357 back around for another shot.

Cade closed the distance. He got close enough to land a second blow across Hap's gun arm with the rifle barrel. Hap's gun discharged harmlessly into the wall. Hap took a step that landed him on several more of the spilled cartridges. He went down with an audible thunk as the back of his head struck the stone fireplace.

For a moment, Cade stood there, swaying in shock. Hap didn't move. The gun had fallen from his limp fingers and his face was bathed in blood from the cut on his forehead. He looked dead.

In the silence, broken only by his own heaving breathing, Cade suddenly heard the sound of gravel crunching beneath tires. A car was tearing up the drive.

Ignoring the hot pain in his side and chest, Cade skirted the spilled cartridges and reached inside the gun cabinet for the other box of rifle shells. He was stuffing them into the chamber as he ran for the back door. Unfortunately, the kidnappers had made excellent time.

He circled around the back of the house. The only chance was to get them once they were out of the car. He was no marksman, especially not with a rifle.

Hap's horse, Fijo, stood on the far side of the house out of sight, calmly lipping grass. He whickered softly and Cade patted the bay gently, easing past.

The kidnappers were already out of the car when he reached the front edge of the house. The bigger man held Jayne tightly in front of him, the gun pressed against her neck. Even from this angle, Cade saw an ugly bruise forming across her cheek. He clenched the rifle and his jaw as they hauled her toward the door. She had to run to keep up with the man. She was wearing a dress and a pair of very high heels.

Her gaze darted wildly from side to side. Cade stepped back, not sure if she saw him, but unwilling to be seen by the two thugs before they got a lot closer.

He needed a clear shot. Jayne was in the way. Cautiously, he stuck his head around the house again. Jayne sagged abruptly. The action pulled her free of the shorter man. Even the big guy let go for that split instant, barking an order at her. Both men's attention was firmly on her and Jayne was down and out of his way. Cade fired.

And missed.

The men spun toward him. Jayne stepped down hard with her pointy heel on the shorter man's instep. Then she launched her weight against the one who'd been holding her. He staggered back against the house, his shot going wide. Jayne sprinted away, running toward the car. Cade fired rapidly to cover her. He didn't care if he hit them. Until the shorter man turned his gun toward Jayne's fleeing form.

Cade aimed and fired. The man screamed, a high shrill sound that sent chills racing down Cade's spine. But that didn't stop either man from returning fire. Cade ducked back behind the edge of the house. Fijo nickered at his back.

The big guy started in his direction and stopped. The sound of a vehicle roaring across the field drew all of their attention. Rio!

Hap had been wrong. The men hadn't waited for him

at all. Nor did the two thugs wait now. Guns blazing in Cade's direction, they started toward their car. The pickup truck was still some distance away.

Cade heard the front door of the house open. Lou turned and fired. Hap staggered forward. He collapsed on the porch, the .357 still clutched in his hand.

The two men reached their car. Cade held his fire because he'd lost track of Jayne. He'd last seen her dart behind the dark sedan. There was too much danger of shooting and hitting her if he wasn't careful.

As if summoned, she appeared, inching around the back of the car. The thugs hadn't spotted her yet, but she saw Cade. She looked at him and raised her hand. Sunlight glinted on the metal wiggling from her fingers. She'd taken their keys from the ignition!

Cade grinned and started forward.

"Frank! The girl musta took the keys!"

Frank leaned against the car. Blood stained his pant leg. "Get us out of here, Lou! They're coming!"

Fijo butted Cade in the back, startling him. As if that were a signal, Jayne suddenly sprinted from behind the car and raced toward him. She'd kicked off her high heels, but Cade knew she'd never make it.

Everything began to happen in slow motion. Cade grabbed the pommel and swung onto Fijo's back. He spurred the big bay forward.

Lou took a second to put a new clip in his gun. Then he brought the weapon up and began running after Jayne, firing wildly.

Cade moved Fijo between Jayne and Lou, and Lou's gun jammed. With a curse, he began running in the opposite direction. Cade dropped the useless rifle. He reached for the rope instead and did what he did best.

Fijo responded like the well-trained cutting horse he

was. As Cade coiled the rope and let it fly, man and horse worked as a team. The rope settled over Lou as perfectly as a man could ask.

Cade pulled up the slack, bringing Lou to his knees, his arms pinned at his sides. The gun dropped from his hand. Rushing forward, Cade trussed the hapless felon tighter than any steer he'd ever roped. And if his boot and his fist connected several times with enough force to shatter Lou's jaw, well, maybe the bastard would think twice before he hit a woman again. It was certainly well worth the new pain running up his arm.

"Hey…Cade…" Rio panted, running up. "Nice work."

"And my time wasn't bad, either," Cade said, pleased with himself as he stood back and twisted to find Jayne.

She was standing a few yards away. She'd picked up his rifle and was holding it on Frank. Cade wondered if she realized the rifle was empty. Obviously, Frank didn't. He slumped in the dirt beside the car, his gun now several feet away. Blood soaked his pant leg and began to pool in the dirt of the yard.

One of Cade's men hurried forward, his own gun ready.

"Watch this bastard. If he moves, shoot him and save the state the cost of a trial," Cade ordered.

Another of his men sprinted to where Jayne stood. Jayne handed him the rifle and ran to meet Cade halfway. She stopped just short of his reaching arms, her eyes wide with horror.

"You're bleeding!"

Her words were an invitation to the fiery tide of pain that had been pushed aside by the adrenaline rush.

"Wish you hadn't reminded me. I hope you won't

think any less of me, but I don't think I'm gonna handle being shot quite as well as you did."

"Rio! I need help," she yelled as his legs began to buckle.

She came under his arm, taking some of the weight off his uncertain legs. Funny. Now that all the shooting was over, they'd turned to rubber on him.

"Sheriff's comin' up the drive," someone yelled.

"Don't imagine he's going to be any too happy with us, either," Cade muttered. He leaned his face into the silken spill of her hair and closed his eyes.

"Grab him, Rio, I can't hold him."

"I've got him."

Cade felt Rio's tough wiry strength on his other side. He wanted to protest, but the world kept trying to fade away.

"Get him over there by the truck. We've got to stop this bleeding."

Sounded like a good idea to Cade. He opened his eyes and saw Hap lying outside the front door where he'd fallen. Coming up the driveway he spotted Sheriff Beaufort and a state police car.

"Oh, man. Look over there! Hap's been shot. Somebody get to Hap!" Rio yelled, obviously spotting the other man for the first time.

"Don't worry about him," Jayne said brusquely. "He's the one who was behind all the trouble here on the Circle M."

"Hap?" Rio said incredulously.

Cade smiled inside. Leave it to Jayne to figure out the truth.

"Yes, Hap. That is, if his last name is Ramirez."

"Yeah. It is."

"Luís told Zed and me he was helping Hap cause havoc here on the ranch."

They came to a stop and Cade felt her hand pushing a curl of hair off his forehead. He felt the fine tremor in her fingers.

"Those two thugs shot Zed."

Cade opened his eyes. "He'll be okay. He called to warn me."

He bit back a groan as Rio and Jayne eased him onto the truck's tailgate.

"Don't try to talk. You're losing so much blood."

Jayne's worried features filled his gaze. He liked that she was worried about him, but the sight of her bruised face made him want to stand up and walk back over to Frank and Lou and do some more permanent damage. Unfortunately, he was pretty sure standing was no longer an option. The way his chest felt, breathing wasn't such a great option, either.

Jayne was ripping at his shirt to get at his bare chest. Too bad it was because he was wounded. He'd always wondered what it would be like to have a woman tear his clothes off. The thought made him smile, even as the world seemed to dim a little more.

"Oh, God!"

He glanced down and saw the path the bullet had cut across his chest. "At least it didn't penetrate," he managed to say. "Hap's as bad a shot…as those lousy baby-nappers."

"Hap shot you? That bastard!"

"But why would Hap shoot Cade?" Rio asked, puzzled.

"Didn't someone say he wanted Cade's ranch?" Jayne asked as she reached under her dress and shimmied out of a nylon half slip.

Rio looked away quickly, a dull flush staining his cheeks. Jayne didn't seem concerned at all as she used the slip to apply pressure to Cade's bleeding wound.

"Cade wouldn't sell," she continued, her worried eyes raking him. "Am I right?"

"Not…'til I met you," he agreed.

Puzzled, she stared at him, but before she could ask, Rio interrupted.

"What should we tell them?" He indicated the approaching cars.

"Anything…they want…to know." Cade whistled between his teeth as the pain spread.

"Shh. Stop trying to talk. Send them to me, Rio. I'll handle it."

Cade smiled, despite the pain. "Better…listen to her, Rio. If I'm real lucky…we'll all be doin' it…from now on."

Her body stilled. He tried to say more, but it was such a tremendous effort. He closed his eyes again.

"Cade! Cade! Stay with me. Do you hear me?"

"Bossy," he murmured. "Not…dead yet."

"And you aren't going to die, is that clear?"

Cade knew his smile widened. She loved him whether she knew it or not. Hap had done him a favor after all. Now he wouldn't have to work so hard to find the words. Maybe he could work it so she was the one who did the proposing.

"Wouldn't…dream…of…"

Epilogue

Cade strode over to the hospital bed where Zed lay.

"How are you doing?"

"Ready to get out of here. How about you?"

"They released me last night."

Zed's eyebrows reached for his forehead. "And you came back?"

"Thought I'd check on you."

"Yeah? Thanks. How's Jayne?"

Cade pulled up a chair, hoping his expression was as blank as the white sheets on Zed's bed. "I don't know, I haven't seen her."

Zed muttered something under his breath that Cade decided he was better off not hearing.

"She was here last night," Zed told him.

"Here? To see you?"

"That depends." Zed eyed him warily. "If I say yes are you gonna hit me? 'Cause I gotta tell you, Cade, I'm not up to going a round with a housefly just yet."

He'd lost hours thanks to the drugs and the blood loss, but Cade hadn't lost his memory. They had told him Jayne had stayed until the nurses threw her out. And he remembered her sitting beside his hospital bed, demanding that he live, and talking about one subject after another till her voice grew hoarse. He'd managed to open his eyes long enough to focus on the face he'd come to love.

"I love you, you foolish, stubborn man," she'd whispered, a sheen of tears in her eyes. He'd slept deeply after that, believing that promise. Only she hadn't returned yesterday and they'd sent him home with Rio to his grandfather's empty house.

"You two are a pair," Zed told him with a shake of his head.

"Keep it in mind," Cade told him.

Zed managed a cocky smile. He still looked wan and drawn after his ordeal. He hadn't been as lucky as Cade. The bullet had punctured his lung and torn up a few things inside as well. The doctor still had him hooked to an IV drip. Cade's bullet had skimmed the surface, tearing away skin and tissue, but nothing that wouldn't heal in time.

"The lady is all yours, Cade," Zed assured him. "She doesn't want me. Hell, I'm not sure she even likes me."

"You saved her life, twice."

"So did you."

"She hasn't called."

And he hadn't meant to say that.

"So you called her, right?" Zed rubbed his eyes with his large hand and shook his head again. "Of course you didn't. What was I thinking?"

"She's young."

"She's gorgeous."

Cade glared at him. Zed chuckled again.

"Her dad offered me a job," Zed told him.

Jealousy reared its ugly head. Cade squashed it back to the dark corners of his mind. "Going to take it?"

"A man's gotta work."

"You could work for me. With Hap dead, I'm going to need a new foreman."

"What about Rio?"

"I gave him a raise."

"Well, I wouldn't want to work for you and have to worry what you'd be thinkin' every time Jayne said hello to me."

"You're making the assumption she'd be around," Cade said.

"If she isn't, you really are dumber than mud. How can you be such a fool?"

"I'm not real good with words." Cade hesitated. "If I was, I'd be able to swallow my pride and apologize to you. Jayne told me how Bonita set you up. Guess I am dumber than mud. I should have figured it out for myself."

Zed's posture relaxed. "Bonita was good at tying a man in knots."

"Yeah."

"Jayne's nothing like Bonita."

"I know that."

"You want some advice? Go see her. You'll find the words. And Cade, I'd better be godfather to your first-born or I'm gonna be unhappy."

Something inside him loosened. This was Zed. He should have trusted him a long time ago. "How about best man?"

Zed grinned. "Give me a date and time."

"I have to get her to say yes, first."

"Do that."

JAYNE CALLED encouragement to the young foster child who was circling the training ring on Sandusty Sun. The young girl's eyes sparkled with excitement as she guided the gelding around the circle all by herself for the first time.

H. L. Bateman moved up to stand beside his daughter. "Carlita's doing real well."

"I think so. She has some natural talent."

"And a good teacher."

Jayne glanced at her father. "Something bothering you?"

"I was just wondering if you'd made that young man of yours suffer enough yet."

"Cade?"

What was her father talking about? She wasn't making Cade McGovern suffer.

"He called a few minutes ago. Wanted to leave you his cell phone number."

Her heart raced. He'd finally called. When she'd gone to the hospital last night and found out he'd already been released, she'd been hurt. Zed had to remind her that Cade wasn't used to having anyone to turn to.

"It's gonna take a little time for him to get it through that thick skull of his that you two are a team," Zed told her.

"He thinks I'm too young."

"So prove him wrong."

"Jayne?"

She looked up and found her father watching her, a wry smile playing around his lips. "Do you want the number?"

"Cade doesn't have a cell phone."

"He does now."

Jayne closed her eyes briefly then remembered to yell encouragement to her young charge. "Doing real good, Carlita." The child beamed.

"Lily Garrett also called," her father resumed. "Something about an invitation. She wants you to call her back. She still trying to get you to go to work for Finders Keepers?"

"Yes, but I told her I wasn't interested. I'm not going back to private investigations."

"Amen to that," he said fervently. "Your mother and your brothers will be vastly relieved."

"So will I," a low voice drawled.

Her body tingled in awareness even before Jayne turned around to find Cade watching her from beneath his lowered hat brim. Her heart soared. She glanced tentatively at her father, who regarded her with a knowing look on his face. "You two talk," he said. "You can make the introductions later. I'll finish up with Carlita." Then he left them to join the young girl in the training ring.

Cade looked strong and powerful and as sexy as the first time Jayne had seen him. She absorbed every nuance of his presence, trying to curb the overpowering urge to fling herself into his arms.

"Hello, cowgirl."

He lifted the brim of his hat with the back of his knuckle. He studied her as if he'd never seen her before. Jayne was acutely conscious of her worn, too tight jeans, and the faded knit shirt that clung to her chest like a second skin.

"Hi, yourself. I heard they released you yesterday."

"Uh-huh. What happened to your hair?"

She touched the short pixie cut and flushed. "I thought cutting my hair would give me a more sophisticated look." Instead, her brother the horse trainer told her she looked like a mischievous elf.

"Now what wicked person told you that?" Cade asked.

He hadn't come one step closer, but somehow the entire world had been reduced to just the two of them and the crazy beating of her heart.

"You hate it."

He closed the distance between them without seeming to move. He reached out and touched her hair. "Actually, it suits you. It's cute."

"I was going for sophisticated."

He stood close enough to touch and her hands itched to do exactly that, but there was pain in his eyes.

"Because of me?"

"Of course not. Should you be out of bed right now?"

His shoulders rose and fell and his hand dropped to her good shoulder. "Probably not. Want to take me home and play nurse? Seems to me, it's my turn to be the cranky patient."

Her hand rose. She stopped it just short of stroking his face. He'd shaved recently. There were several small nicks that needed soothing. Her fingers trembled with the desire to do just that.

"Who are you calling cranky?" she demanded.

His eyes seemed to smile in response. "How's your shoulder?" he asked.

"Healing just fine thanks to you. What about your ribs?"

"I think you should have a look. I don't trust those doctors."

The sensual message was coming through loud and clear. Her body yearned to answer that summons, but she held her ground. This was too important. He had to be sure. If he couldn't put the past behind him, there could be no future.

"Who *do* you trust?" she asked.

"You."

Her heart fluttered to a halt.

"Always."

Breathing was no longer a simple, undirected operation. She remembered to inhale—finally. Her hand reached out to touch his arm before she could hold it still.

"And Zed," he added. "I trust him enough to ask him to be my foreman today."

She released the breath on a whoosh of air. "You did?"

"I may be stubborn—and dense as a horse in a patch of locoweed—but I am trainable." His gaze held hers, baring his uncertainties for her to see. "That is, if someone is willing to take the time."

She couldn't swallow and she couldn't look away. "You said I was too young."

"So maybe I'll have to train you as well."

"Think so?"

His smile came slowly. It started in his eyes and lifted the corners of his mouth until it was wide and sexy and perfect.

"It'll be fun finding out, don't you think?"

She resisted every impulse in her that longed to kiss those lips and plaster herself against that hard lean body. "I think you need to spell it out for me, Cade."

"I was afraid of that. I told Zed I was no good with words."

"You talked to Zed about us?"

"And Rio and Luís and your father and everyone else who would listen."

"Luís?"

Cade shrugged. "His mother died a couple of months ago. He's totally alone now."

"And you know what that feels like." She hurt for the shadows in his eyes.

"We got to talking when I ran into him at the hospital. He went there to thank Zed for saving his life."

"You didn't press charges."

"It would only have been malicious mischief at most. Hap was behind the majority of the damage. Besides, Luís apologized for his part in things. He offered to work for me for free to make up for the fences and the girths and the things he'd had a part in."

"And you're going to let him, aren't you?"

His shoulders inched up a notch.

"The kid doesn't have anyone else. Hap was filling his head with all kinds of tales, but I think deep down he knew what his sister was. Bonita wasn't much of a wife, but that still makes the kid my family in a way. And the rodeo's no life for someone like him. He's bright. Likes computers. I figured maybe he could help me computerize some of my breeding programs and I could help him go to college and—umph"

She launched herself into his arms, forgetting about his injury. When he grunted she would have pulled back only he held her there and covered her mouth with his own.

The universe tilted away. She strained against him, trying to get closer.

"He'd better be planning to marry her," a familiar voice said to her left, "or I'm going to have to forget I'm an officer of the court and beat that cowboy into prime manure."

"I'll help," her brother, the sheriff, agreed.

"Count me in," her brother the trainer said solemnly.

Jayne allowed their lips to cling for a moment longer before reluctantly pulling back to find they'd acquired quite an audience. Her father still stood in the training ring, but her mother was now wrapped in his arms. They were both smiling in her direction. Carlita had stopped riding. The young girl was watching the scene with interest. Jayne's three brothers formed a united semicircle to her left, a few steps from Cade.

"You'd better come and meet my brothers," she said in resignation.

Cade glanced at the three men but he didn't release her. He smiled. "Maybe later. We have a wedding to plan," he said softly.

"We do?"

"Don't we?"

"I guess that depends."

"On?"

"On why you want to marry me."

"Well, I could say it was because the sex was fantastic," he said too softly for her brothers to hear, "but then your brothers would definitely turn me into manure."

She stifled a giggle, but her heart lightened until she thought he might have to hold her just to keep her feet on the ground.

"I could tell you that I was thinking about selling the Circle M and finding a place closer to town and I need you to manage my household."

"You wouldn't sell the Circle M! Oh, Cade, no. It's so beautiful there."

Cade grinned. "Okay. Then I could tell you that I plan to build a new house up where that line shack is and I want it to have a woman's touch."

She knew he felt her tremble. Excitement, desire, longing all jumbled together inside her.

"That would be a great place to have a house."

Cade nodded.

"Or I could simply tell you that my life is totally empty if you aren't part of it." He cupped her face lightly, his eyes dark with need. "I love you, Jayne."

She didn't know if he moved or she did, but the kiss was deeper, stealing her soul.

"I like that reason best," she said against his mouth when she could speak again.

"Me, too. Will you marry me?"

Her smile felt wide enough to light the world. "We could be in Nevada in a matter of hours."

"You are not eloping with our sister," Devlin stated in his most sherifflike tone.

"Better believe it," Liam, the judge, agreed solemnly.

"What's the penalty for aggravated assault, Liam?" Rory, the trainer, asked.

She'd forgotten her brothers were expected today. Apparently, they had arrived. Cade turned slowly, taking her with him. He faced the three men, glanced at her parents and nodded slightly in greeting, before turning back to her brothers.

"I'm not used to having a family," he told the men. "I don't know the way things are done, so I figure we'll have to work out the pecking order later. Right now, your sister and I need some privacy to discuss our plans. So if you'll excuse us?"

"And if we won't?" Rory demanded.

Jayne started to respond, but Cade gave her arm a gentle squeeze.

"Then I'll turn your sister loose on the lot of you," he said calmly.

Jayne felt the laughter bubble up in her chest. She wondered if a person could explode from sheer happiness.

"Aw, hell, not that," Devlin protested.

Liam and Rory grinned. "Poor dumb bastard has no idea what he's in for, does he?" Liam asked.

"Hey, let's not queer this deal or we'll have to keep pulling her out of scrapes ourselves," Rory pointed out. "He looks competent. Let him ride herd on her."

"Good point." Devlin turned toward his parents. "Hey Mom, what's for dinner?"

Jayne and Cade were laughing when they reached the red truck. Cade handed her up and came around to the driver's side, wincing slightly as he got in behind the wheel.

"Are you okay?" she asked.

"I will be, for as long as you love me."

"Then you'd better plan on a long happy life, Cade, because I don't ever plan to stop loving you."

Cade put the truck in gear.

* * * * *

The **TRUEBLOOD, TEXAS** *story continues next month. Don't miss*

SECRET BODYGUARD

by B.J. Daniels.
Turn the page for a sneak peek!

Chapter One

She'd sneak out tonight. He could feel it, the way he always could. A kind of static in the air. Something electric. Something both reckless and dangerous.

Jesse rubbed the cloth over the thin coat of wax on the hood of the black Lincoln. Reflections danced in the shine at his touch. He avoided his own reflection though, his gaze on the massive main house across the Texas tiled courtyard.

The curtains were closed in her window, but the air-conditioned breeze on the other side teased them coyly open allowing him to catch glimpses of her.

It was just like Amanda to have the window open in her wing of the air-conditioned hacienda. No wonder her scent moved restlessly through the hot, humid night. Tantalizing. Tempting. He breathed it in, holding it deep inside him as long as he could before reluctantly releasing it. Her music also drifted from her open window and hung in the thick air between the house and the chauffeur's quarters above the garage. She had the radio on the local Latin station she listened to, the music as hot and spicy as the food she liked to eat.

He rubbed his large hand over the dark, slick hood,

wondering if her skin felt like this. Smooth and cool to the touch.

When she came out, it was through the side door. He stepped back into the shadows, not wanting her to see him. At first he thought she'd take the new Mercedes her father had given her for her twenty-fifth birthday, but she headed for the separate garage on the far side of the house. He watched her stick to the shadows and climb into the older-model BMW parked in the first stall.

Slumming it tonight?

He waited until she'd pulled away, her taillights disappearing down the long, circuitous, tree-arched drive of the Crowe estate before he climbed on his motorcycle and followed her at a discreet distance.

Hidden cameras recorded all movement in the house and on the grounds, which meant she couldn't leave without being noticed. And yet the guard in the small stone building at the edge of the property that acted as the hub of the Crowe's all-encompassing, high-tech security system didn't turn as she breezed past. Nor did he seem to notice Jesse not far behind her.

Before she even got to the massive wrought-iron gate that kept the rest of the world out of the sequestered compound, the gate swung open wide as if she were the princess of the palace. Which, of course, she was.

He barely slipped through behind her before the gate slammed closed, staying just close enough on his bike as she headed for Dallas, that he didn't lose her.

Night air rushed by thick and hot as he wove in and out of the traffic along the outskirts of the Big D, keeping her in sight ahead of him, just as he had all the other nights.

Only tonight felt different. Tonight, after all his waiting, something was going to happen. He sensed it, more aware of the woman he tailed than ever before. He couldn't still the small thrill of secret pleasure that coursed through him. His heart beat a little faster.

Ahead, Amanda pulled over along a dark, nearly isolated street. He swung in behind a pickup parked at the curb and watched her get out. She glanced around as if worried she might have been followed. As if she had something to hide. He smiled to himself. Oh, she had something to hide all right.

Down the block, bright red-and-yellow neon flashed in front of one of those late-night, out-of-the-way Tex-Mex cafés found in this part of Dallas. She walked toward it.

He waited until she was almost there before he pulled his bike back onto the street. As he cruised by, he saw her go to an outside table and sit down with a woman he'd never seen before.

At the end of the block, he turned down the alley and ditched the bike to work his way back toward the café on foot, running on adrenaline, anticipation and enough fear to know he hadn't lost his mind.

He found a spot to watch her from the shadows, close enough he could see but not hear what was being said. She was crying. He could see that, crying and talking hurriedly, nervously. He'd give anything to hear what she was saying and wondered when his heart had grown so cold, so calculating. Mostly, why he believed that Amanda Crowe was lying.

FREE BOOK OFFER!

In August, an exciting new *Maitland Maternity* single title comes with a FREE BOOK attached to it!

Maitland Maternity THE INHERITANCE

by Marie Ferrarella

This brand-new single title revisits all the excitement and characters that you've enjoyed in the *Maitland Maternity* continuity series—but there's more! As part of this extraordinary offer, the first title in Harlequin's new *Trueblood, Texas* continuity will be shrink-wrapped to the *Maitland Maternity* book absolutely FREE! An amazing "2-for-1" value that will introduce you to the wonderful adventure and romance of

TRUEBLOOD, TEXAS

On sale in August 2001 at your favorite retail outlet.

HARLEQUIN®

Makes any time special ®

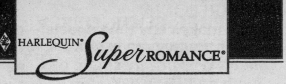

HARLEQUIN *Super*ROMANCE®

To celebrate the
1000th Superromance book
We're presenting you with 3 books
from 3 of your favorite authors in

All Summer Long

Home, Hearth and Haley
by **Muriel Jensen**

Meet the men and women of Muriel's
upcoming **Men of Maple Hill** trilogy

Daddy's Girl
by **Judith Arnold**

Another **Daddy School** story!

Temperature Rising
by **Bobby Hutchinson**

Life and love at St. Joe's Hospital are as feverish
as ever in this **Emergency!** story

On sale July 2001
Available wherever Harlequin books are sold.

HARLEQUIN®
Makes any time special ®

USA Today bestselling author

STELLA CAMERON

and popular American Romance author

MURIEL JENSEN

come together in a special
Harlequin 2-in-1 collection.

Look for

Shadows and *Daddy in Demand*

On sale June 2001

HARLEQUIN®
Makes any time special ®

Harlequin invites you to walk down the aisle...

To honor our year long celebration of weddings, we are offering an exciting opportunity for you to own the Harlequin Bride Doll. Handcrafted in fine bisque porcelain, the wedding doll is dressed for her wedding day in a cream satin gown accented by lace trim. She carries an exquisite traditional bridal bouquet and wears a cathedral-length dotted Swiss veil. Embroidered flowers cascade down her lace overskirt to the scalloped hemline; underneath all is a multi-layered crinoline.

Join us in our celebration of weddings by sending away for your own Harlequin Bride Doll. This doll regularly retails for $74.95 U.S./approx. $108.68 CDN. One doll per household. Requests must be received no later than December 31, 2001. Offer good while quantities of gifts last. Please allow 6-8 weeks for delivery. Offer good in the U.S. and Canada only. Become part of this exciting offer!

**Simply complete the order form and mail to:
"A Walk Down the Aisle"**

IN U.S.A
P.O. Box 9057
3010 Walden Ave.
Buffalo, NY 14269-9057

IN CANADA
P.O. Box 622
Fort Erie, Ontario
L2A 5X3

Enclosed are eight (8) proofs of purchase found in the last pages of every specially marked Harlequin series book and $3.75 check or money order (for postage and handling). Please send my Harlequin Bride Doll to:

_____
Name (PLEASE PRINT)

_____
Address   Apt. #

_____
City   State/Prov.   Zip/Postal Code

_____
Account # (if applicable)   **097 KIK DAEW**

Visit us at www.eHarlequin.com

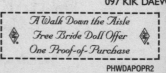

A Walk Down the Aisle
Free Bride Doll Offer
One Proof-of-Purchase

PHWDAPOPR2